EMERGING ISSUES IN PUBLIC HEALTH

Gun Violence

Bradley Steffens

San Diego, CA

About the Author

Bradley Steffens is a poet, a novelist, and an award-winning author of more than forty nonfiction books for children and young adults.

© 2020 ReferencePoint Press, Inc.
Printed in the United States

For more information, contact:
ReferencePoint Press, Inc.
PO Box 27779
San Diego, CA 92198
www.ReferencePointPress.com

ALL RIGHTS RESERVED.
No part of this work covered by the copyright hereon may be reproduced or used in any form or by any means—graphic, electronic, or mechanical, including photocopying, recording, taping, web distribution, or information storage retrieval systems—without the written permission of the publisher.

LIBRARY OF CONGRESS CATALOGING-IN-PUBLICATION DATA

Name: Steffens, Bradley, 1955– author.
Title: Gun Violence/by Bradley Steffens.
Description: San Diego, CA: ReferencePoint Press, Inc., 2020. | Series: Emerging Issues in Public Health | Includes bibliographical references and index. |
Identifiers: LCCN 2018058354 (print) | LCCN 2019002185 (ebook) | ISBN 9781682826706 (eBook) | ISBN 9781682826690 (hardback)
Subjects: LCSH: Firearms ownership—Health aspects—United States—Juvenile literature. | Gunshot wounds—United States—Juvenile literature. | Gun control—United States—Juvenile literature. | Public health—United States—Juvenile literature.
Classification: LCC HV7436 (ebook) | LCC HV7436 .S749 2020 (print) | DDC 363.330973—dc23
LC record available at https://lccn.loc.gov/2018058354

CONTENTS

Introduction A Deadly Epidemic	4
Chapter One The Making of a Crisis	8
Chapter Two When Gun Violence Becomes Commonplace	19
Chapter Three Guns and Suicide	30
Chapter Four The Human Toll of Gun Violence	41
Chapter Five What Is Being Done to Reduce Gun Violence?	52
Source Notes	65
Organizations and Websites	70
For Further Research	73
Index	75
Picture Credits	80

INTRODUCTION

A Deadly Epidemic

At 7:30 a.m. on May 18, 2018, seventeen-year-old Dimitrios Pagourtzis, a student at Santa Fe High School in Santa Fe, Texas, walked into the school's art complex armed with a .38 caliber pistol and a pump-action shotgun and began shooting his classmates. When teachers tried stop him, he shot them as well. By the time Pagourtzis surrendered to police thirty minutes later, eight students and two teachers lay dead.

It was a grim day of gun violence, but it had only started. Just thirteen minutes later, a man got out of his car at a Kwik Trip convenience store in Sauk City, Wisconsin, and shot himself in the parking lot—a suicide.

The gun violence continued throughout the day. In Marrero, Louisiana, forty-four-year-old Christopher Pike and forty-three-year-old Melissa Baous went to the home of forty-four-year-old Tonia Dardar to resolve a property dispute. The three argued, and Pike shot and killed the two women. When Dardar's husband came home, he confronted Pike. The two exchanged gunfire. Pike suffered fatal wounds and died at the scene. In Chicago, Illinois, at 5:29 p.m., forty-seven-year-old Erica Frazier was standing on a street corner talking with a forty-six-year-old man when a male teenager approached them with a gun and fired. The man was wounded in the leg and survived. Frazier, who was shot in the torso, died. Later that evening, in Gresham, Oregon, twenty-four-year-old Dmitri Bullard charged toward two police officers with a hatchet. The officers fired their weapons at Bullard, killing him.

Unfortunately, that was not the end of the day's violence. In Tulsa, Oklahoma, a fifteen-year-old boy shot his seventeen-year-old brother in the head with a gun he thought was unloaded. In Greensboro, North Carolina, two armed men staged a home invasion. One of the home owners, Pamela Crumpton Hooks, age thirty-four, was shot and killed.

In all, forty-four people died from gunshot wounds in the United States on May 18, 2018, and seventy-five were injured. The oldest was seventy-one; the youngest, fifteen. They are all deeply missed by family and friends. "I have no words . . . such an amazing person and mother inside and out. Gone too soon!"[1] wrote one person on Hooks's online memorial page. "I worked with Pam," wrote another. "She was a very kind and generous lady. Gone but not forgotten."[2] A third wrote, "I miss you already my friend. You were an amazing mom. Love you!"[3] No one knows what the shooting victims might have become, what they might have accomplished, or how they might have changed the world. One might have cured a disease; another might have created a great work of art; another might have led his or her community, state, or country. But no more. All of their potential is gone. Only their memories are left.

> "I have no words . . . such an amazing person and mother inside and out. Gone too soon!"[1]
>
> —A friend of gun violence victim Pamela Crumpton Hooks

The Unthinkable Has Become Commonplace

May 18, 2018, was a horrific day for gun violence, but it was not unusual. In fact, the very next day, May 19, 2018, forty-two people died in the United States from gunshot wounds, and one hundred were injured—and there was no mass shooting that day. And so it goes, day after day, month after month, year after year. In 2015 the number of firearm deaths surpassed the number of traffic deaths for the first time, becoming the second-leading cause of injury death in the United States. In all, there were 39,773 deaths from firearms in the United States in 2017—an average of 109 people a day. It is the equivalent of a jumbo

US Gun Deaths Surge to Fifty-Year High

In 2017 firearm-related deaths surged to the highest level in fifty years, according to a 2018 report from the Centers for Disease Control and Prevention (CDC). It was the third consecutive year of dramatic increases in gun deaths in the United States. The number of deaths per 100,000 people also increased markedly. After remaining steady at about 10.3 gun deaths per 100,000 people throughout the 2000s, the rate jumped to 11.8 per 100,000 in 2016 and then to 12.0 per 100,000 in 2017.

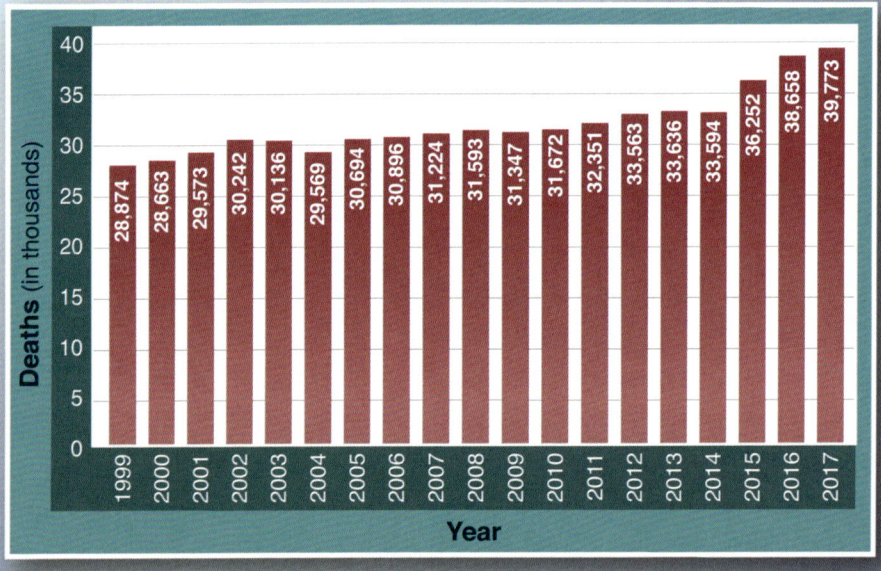

Source: Centers for Disease Control and Prevention, "Underlying Cause of Death, 1999–2017 Results," 2018. https://wonder.cdc.gov.

jet full of passengers crashing every four days. But if that many planes were crashing, it would be a national crisis. Flights would be grounded. Everything would come to a halt to find out what was killing so many people. But for most people, gunshot deaths are just a statistic, something political leaders and the media discuss only before elections or after mass killings.

The reason for this is simple. Gun violence does not have a single cause that can be easily addressed. Instead it has many underlying causes. For example, 60 percent of firearm deaths are suicides, which is itself an epidemic with many different causes. Some gun deaths are the result of criminal activity. Others result from domestic violence, and still others fall under the category of workplace violence. Each of these causes is different from the others and requires different remedies. Describing it in medical terms, David Studdert, a professor of medicine and law at Stanford University, says, "Gun violence is not one epidemic, but several sub-epidemics, each with very different properties and racial profiles. . . . These different sub-epidemics clearly call for different policy responses."[4]

Firearm injury is the third-leading cause of death among US children ages seventeen and younger, and it is the leading cause of death among African American teens ages fifteen to nineteen. Whether it is a single epidemic or many subepidemics, gun violence is a public health crisis.

> "Gun violence is not one epidemic, but several sub-epidemics, each with very different properties and racial profiles. . . . These different sub-epidemics clearly call for different policy responses."[4]
>
> —David Studdert, a professor of medicine and law at Stanford University

CHAPTER ONE

The Making of a Crisis

More people die from gunshot wounds in the United States than in any other country in the world except Brazil. This is the finding of a 2018 study published in the *Journal of the American Medical Association* (*JAMA*) by researchers at the University of Washington's Institute for Health Metrics and Evaluation. The United States is the world's third-largest country by population, so it is not surprising that it would rank near the top of all nations in the number of deaths from any cause. But the United States has a much higher number of firearm deaths per 100,000 people—the common way to measure the frequency of death and disease among populations—than most other countries do. The rate of firearm deaths in the United States is 12.0 per 100,000 people, according to a 2017 study done by the Centers for Disease Control and Prevention (CDC). That is more than four times higher than the world's second-most populous country, India, which has a rate of 2.6 per 100,000.

The difference in firearm mortality rates is even greater when the United States is compared with countries with similar levels of governmental stability and economic development. The US firearm mortality rate is six times higher than that of its next-door neighbor, Canada (2.1 per 100,000). It is thirteen times higher than that of Germany (0.9 per 100,000). And it is an astonishing forty times higher than that of the United Kingdom (0.3 per 100,000). "It is a little surprising that a country like ours should have this level of gun violence," says Ali Mokdad, a professor of global health and epidemiology at the University of Washington's Institute for Health Metrics and Evaluation. "If you compare us to other well-off countries, we really stand out."[5] The United States is the only advanced nation where gun violence is an emerging public health crisis.

Gun Ownership

One of the main reasons why the United States leads the developed world in firearm mortality is that it also leads the world in the number of privately owned firearms. Obviously, if guns are scarce, firearm deaths will be rare. For example, the gun ownership rate in China is just 3.6 guns per every 100 people—thirty-three times lower than the US rate—and its firearm mortality rate is just 0.2 per 100,000 people—fifty times lower than the US rate. If guns are plentiful, as they are in the United States, the number of firearm deaths will be higher. The sheer availability of guns means they can be used more often in suicides, homicides, and defensive acts, all of which contribute to the overall US firearm mortality rate. "We see a fairly consistent relationship, when you control for other factors, the more firearms there are, the greater the risk for both firearm homicide and suicide,"[6] says Daniel W. Webster, director of the Center for Gun Policy and Research at Johns Hopkins University.

> "We see a fairly consistent relationship, when you control for other factors, the more firearms there are, the greater the risk for both firearm homicide and suicide."[6]
>
> —Daniel W. Webster, director of the Center for Gun Policy and Research at Johns Hopkins University

Americans are affluent by global standards and have more money to spend on guns than most people in the world do. US civilians own more than 343 million firearms, according to the 2018 Small Arms Survey, a study conducted by the Graduate Institute of International and Development Studies in Geneva, Switzerland. This amounts to 120.5 firearms for every 100 residents. This is more than ten times higher than the global average of 11.3 firearms for every 100 residents. The United States is the only country in the world where the number of guns exceeds the number of people. Canada, with 34.7 guns for every 100 residents, is a distant second in gun ownership among industrialized countries.

Americans make up 4.2 percent of the world's population yet own 46 percent of the world's privately held firearms.

Not every American owns a gun, of course, but firearms are spread throughout the population in greater numbers than in other countries. According to a March 2018 survey by NBC News and the *Wall Street Journal*, 47 percent of Americans live in a household with a gun. This is far more than any other country. The country with the second-highest level of gun ownership is Switzerland, in which 28.6 percent of households have a gun.

US polls probably underestimate the number of households with guns. This is because pollsters rely on the truthfulness of the people they interview. However, it is unlikely that people in households where someone possesses a stolen gun report having them, and a 2018 study by Harvard found that between three hundred thousand and six hundred thousand guns are stolen every year in the United States. Some lawful gun owners might

Guns are widely available in the United States. People can buy them in gun stores, sporting goods stores, pawn shops, at gun shows, and even online.

deny having guns as well. In 2017 the polling firm Zogby Analytics posed the question, "If a national pollster asked you if you owned a firearm, would you determine to tell him or her the truth or would you feel it was none of their business?"[7] Fully 36 percent of those surveyed said it was none of the pollster's business. Based on the findings by Zogby, it is plausible that most of the people not answering yes or no actually do have a gun, meaning that half of American households probably have a firearm.

The Roots of a Gun Culture

The high level of American gun ownership has many causes. First, guns are widely available. People can buy them at gun stores, sporting goods stores, gun shows, and pawnshops, as well as online. Many guns are given as gifts, especially in rural parts of the country. Other guns are passed down from parents to children. In many families, receiving a gun is a rite of passage into adulthood. Other reasons for gun ownership include personal protection, hunting, collecting, and sport.

Personal protection ranks highest among the reasons for owning a gun, according to a 2017 poll by the Pew Research Center. The pollsters found that 67 percent of gun owners cite protection as their main reason for owning a gun. "The formula is simple: Criminals and the dangerously mentally ill make our nation more violent," writes attorney and journalist David French. "Because I don't want to be dependent on a sometimes shockingly incompetent government for my family's security—I carry a weapon. My wife does as well. We're not scared. We're prepared."[8]

Gun availability alone does not determine the number of gun deaths a country has. Social, legal, and cultural differences are also factors. For example, countries with weak criminal justice systems, such as El Salvador and Venezuela, have exceptionally high rates of firearm homicides. Countries with strong religious institutions tend to have low rates of firearm suicides. Often these differences have a long cultural history. The United States was founded by an armed revolution against the British crown, and guns have figured prominently in its history. "America is the gun," writes *New York Times* columnist Charles M. Blow. "Its very beginning is rooted in gun violence. It is by the barrel that this land was acquired. It is by the barrel that the slave was subdued and his rebellions squashed. And that is to say nothing of our wars."[9]

Few Restrictions

Another reason for the widespread ownership of guns in the United States is that there are few legal restrictions to owning one. Under federal law a person has to be twenty-one to buy a handgun from a licensed dealer, but the age limit drops to eighteen if the gun is purchased from a private seller. The minimum age to purchase a long gun, or rifle, from a licensed dealer is eighteen under federal law. However, there is no federal minimum age to purchase a rifle from a private seller at a gun show, yard sale, or flea market or through an advertisement. In addition, unlike operating a motor vehicle, there is no age limit on using a gun. If a parent wants to lend or give a child a gun and take him or her hunting or target shooting, there is no law prohibiting it.

Some states have stricter age limits than under federal law. California, Florida, Hawaii, and Illinois limit the sales of long guns to those who are twenty-one or older. Fifteen states have raised the minimum age for buying a handgun from a private seller to twenty-one. No states restrict the possession or use of firearms by minors.

Federal law does prohibit some people from purchasing guns on the basis of their criminal history or mental health. The Brady Handgun Violence Prevention Act of 1993 prohibits the purchase of a gun by any person who has been convicted of a crime punishable by imprisonment for a term exceeding one year; is a fugitive from justice; has been committed to a mental institution or found by a court to have mental problems; is subject to a court order that restrains him or her from harassing, stalking, or threatening an intimate partner or child of such intimate partner; or has been convicted of domestic violence.

People shop at the Dallas Gun Show in Texas. While you must be eighteen to buy a rifle from a licensed dealer, there is no federal minimum age to purchase these guns from private sellers at gun shows.

To ensure that people prohibited by law from buying guns do not do so, federally licensed gun sellers are required to verify a buyer's identification and run a background check prior to selling the firearm. To do this, the licensed gun dealer contacts the National Instant Criminal Background Check System (NICS), an electronic database maintained by the FBI. Most NICS background checks take only minutes to complete. Since NICS was launched in 1998, the FBI has performed 230 million background checks, leading to more than 1.3 million denials of sales.

Stronger Laws in Canada

Restrictions on gun ownership are weaker in the United States than they are in most advanced countries, and the lack of screening could be one factor in the high US firearm mortality rate. For example, Canadians are required to have a valid license to own and purchase guns. There is no loophole for guns purchased privately or given as gifts. To obtain a gun license, the individual must pass a background check that is tighter than the US background

Nonfatal Firearm Injuries

Most of the attention in the gun violence debate focuses on firearm deaths. However, two-thirds of gunshot victims are not fatally injured. When suicides are excluded, the ratio of nonfatal firearm injuries to fatal injuries is even higher: Six out of every seven people wounded in a shooting survive.

According to the CDC, the number of fatal firearm injuries per 100,000 people increased by 16.5 percent from 2001 to 2017, from 10.3 to 12.0 per 100,000 people, but the number of nonfatal firearm injuries increased a staggering 92 percent, from 21.7 to 41.7 per 100,000. "This country has a real challenge—an epidemic of firearm injury," says Sandro Galea, dean of the Boston University School of Public Health. About 80 percent of gunshot wounds require hospitalization. Despite advanced treatment, many gunshot victims end up having a poor quality of life. In fact, a large number of the wounded later die of health consequences related to the gunshot trauma.

Gunshot wounds scar not only the body but also the mind. "I'm still waiting for my old self to come back," says a woman who sustained a gunshot wound in the arm during an episode of workplace violence fifteen years earlier. Thea James, director of the Violence Intervention Advocacy Program in Boston, says that gunshot wounds are particularly damaging to African American men, who often do not seek psychological help after receiving them. When they later act out or refuse to cooperate with authority figures, "that's not bad behavior," says James, "it's a manifestation of their trauma."

Quoted in David S. Bernstein, "Americans Don't Really Understand Gun Violence," *Atlantic*, December 14, 2017. www.theatlantic.com.

---

check. Applicants also must present third-party character references to the licensing bureau. Significantly, applicants must successfully complete a safety course to be eligible for a license. Finally, a mandatory twenty-eight-day waiting period is imposed on first-time applicants. Measuring the impact of licensing alone is difficult, because Canada has enacted many guns laws since the Firearms Act of 1995, when licensing became a requirement. Nevertheless, Canadian gun homicides reached a fifty-year low in 2013 and remained 15 percent lower in 2016 than they were in 1995, when the licensing law was passed.

Gun licensing like Canada's would seem to address several causes of the gun mortality rate in the United States. For example, the twenty-eight-day waiting period might prevent some firearm suicides, since a certain number of suicides are an impulsive reaction to a temporary crisis, such as the breakup of a relationship or a lost job. The United States does not have national gun licensing and other stronger restrictions because the nation does not have a political consensus on gun policy. According to a 2017 Pew Research Center study, not only do nearly half of American households own a gun, more than half (52 percent) of those who do not own a gun say they could see themselves owning one in the future. The majority of these people do not support further restrictions on legal gun ownership.

Canada has stricter gun control laws than the United States. In Canada, for example, people applying for gun licenses must complete a safety course to be eligible to purchase a firearm.

Many gun rights advocates argue that most gun-related crimes are carried out with stolen and other illegally obtained guns. As a result, new regulations on gun ownership would do little to reduce gun violence. A 2016 study by researchers at the University of Pittsburgh supports this view. The researchers partnered with the Pittsburgh police department to identify the owners of all guns recovered from crime scenes. They found that in 79 percent of the cases, the perpetrator was not a lawful firearm owner but rather was illegally in possession of a gun that belonged to someone else. About 22 percent of those guns were given to the criminal by the lawful owner; 33 percent were stolen, and in 44 percent of the cases, it could not be determined whether the gun was stolen. "All guns start out as legal guns," says Anthony Fabio, an epidemiologist who led the study. "But a huge number of them move into illegal hands. As a public-health person, I'd like to be able to figure out that path."[10] In addition, half of all gun homicides occur in just 2 percent of the nation's counties—mostly urban areas. Many rural states have high gun ownership rates but small numbers of gun homicides. For example, 48.9 percent of Alabama's residents own guns, but the state had only one firearm murder in 2016. Not surprisingly, people in Alabama do not see a pressing need for tougher gun laws.

> "All guns start out as legal guns. But a huge number of them move into illegal hands."[10]
>
> —Anthony Fabio, an epidemiologist at the University of Pittsburgh

A Standoff on Gun Policy

One of the barriers to enacting further gun restrictions is the legislative system of the United States, known as bicameralism. Under this system, new laws must be passed by majorities in two houses; namely, the House of Representatives and the Senate. While members of the House are apportioned on the basis of

System Failure Leads to Tragedy

The National Instant Criminal Background Check System (NICS) is supposed to keep guns out of the hands of people who present a danger to themselves and others. For the system to work, however, law enforcement, criminal justice, and mental health professionals must forward the names and fingerprints of individuals who are barred from owning guns to the FBI. This did not happen in the case of Devin P. Kelley, an air force veteran who was convicted of domestic violence by an air force general court-martial in 2012. The conviction made him ineligible to purchase a firearm, but according to a 2018 report by the US Department of Defense, the air force missed four opportunities to submit Kelley's fingerprints and two opportunities to send a report of his conviction to the FBI as required by policies. "The failures had drastic consequences and should not have occurred," the inspector general's report concluded. Because Kelley's name and fingerprints were not in the NICS database, Kelley was able to purchase four firearms, including a semiautomatic military-style assault rifle.

On November 5, 2018, Kelley went to the First Baptist Church in Sutherland Springs, Texas, armed with three of the guns he had legally purchased due to the reporting error. His mother-in-law attended the church, but she was not present at the Sunday morning service when Kelley, dressed in black and wearing a skull-face mask, came into the church, spraying bullets from side to side. He killed twenty-six people, including an eighteen-month-old toddler, before taking his own life.

Quoted in Christopher Mele, "Air Force Missed 6 Chances to Stop Gunman in Texas Church Shooting from Buying Weapons, U.S. Says," *New York Times*, December 7, 2018. www.nytimes.com.

---

each state's population, the Senate comprises two senators from each state. This gives all the states an equal voice in the Senate, regardless of the size of their populations. California, the most populous state, and Wyoming, the least populous state, each have two senators. At the same time, gun ownership is not equal across the states. For example, California, which led the nation in gun homicides in 2016 with 1,368, has a gun ownership rate of only 19 percent. Wyoming, which had the second-fewest gun homicides in 2016 with just six, has a gun ownership rate of 54 percent. Voters in California tend to support gun control laws, while voters in Wyoming oppose them. In the Senate the votes from states with high gun ownership often cancel out the votes from states with low gun ownership, creating a political standoff.

In addition, the Senate allows a minority of senators to block legislation by using an open-ended debate known as a filibuster. Ending a filibuster requires a three-fifths vote in the Senate. Because of the filibuster, no law can pass the Senate without a supermajority of sixty votes. That means that forty-one senators from just twenty-one states with high rates of gun ownership can block gun control legislation in the Senate. Because of this standoff, no new federal gun control legislation has been enacted since the Violent Crime Control and Law Enforcement Act of 1994. In fact, very little gun legislation is even proposed, because the failure of passage is certain even before the process begins.

Gun policy in the United States is also influenced by the National Rifle Association (NRA), a nonprofit organization that advocates for gun rights and opposes many restrictions on gun ownership. During the 2016 elections, the NRA contributed $834,000 to 223 Republicans and 9 Democrats running for Congress. But political contributions are not the main source of the organization's influence, according to Lee Drutman, a senior fellow at the think tank New America. What is important are the organization's 6 million current members and the millions of former members who are still on the organization's email lists. "The donations themselves are clearly not the reason Republican lawmakers fear opposing the NRA—the much bigger threat the gun rights group poses is its ability to mobilize and excite huge numbers of voters,"[11] says Drutman.

Because of the high number of gun owners in many states and their political clout, the United States is likely to remain one of the easiest places to obtain a gun in the world. As a result, it will likely lead the world in both lawful and unlawful gun ownership—and one of the highest rates of gun mortality—for the foreseeable future.

CHAPTER TWO

When Gun Violence Becomes Commonplace

November 13, 2018, was an unseasonably cool day in Houston, Texas, as eighteen-year-old De'Lindsey Dwayne Mack and a female friend walked along the street one block east of the school they attended, Lamar High School. Earlier that day, a light dusting of snow had fallen, the earliest snowfall in the city's history. The beginning of Thanksgiving break was just three days away. Sadly, Mack would not live to see it. At about 12:15 p.m., a dark Subaru sedan pulled up next to Mack and his friend and stopped. A teen wearing a mask and a black hoodie got out of the car and opened fire, wounding Mack and grazing his friend with a bullet. The shooting did not end there. "Once this suspect fired upon the male and female, the male went down," Houston Police Department executive assistant chief Troy Finner later told reporters in a halting voice. "That suspect stood over that individual and fired more shots."[12] A total of twelve rounds were fired.

Police believe the cold-blooded murder was meant to send a message. Mack's murder was preceded by a series of back-and-forth shootings by rival gangs. It turned out to have been a tragic case of mistaken identity. Mack did not belong to a gang but had posted selfies on Instagram that made it appear that he did. "Anybody who knows and knew De'Lindsey would know him to be a big talker, but he was not a gangster,"[13] says Dr. D.Z. Cofield, the pastor at Mack's church and a spokesperson for the family. Nevertheless, Houston police categorized the shooting as gang related since the shooting was motivated by gang rivalry.

Gang violence makes up only 13 percent of all US homicides, according to the FBI, but in some areas the numbers are much higher. In cities such as Los Angeles and Chicago, more than half of all homicides are gang related. Gang homicides are especially prevalent among persons aged fifteen to twenty-four, accounting for up to 69 percent of homicides among persons in this age group in some cities. In part because of gang violence, homicide is the third-leading cause of death among persons aged fifteen to twenty-four in the United States, according to the Centers for Disease Control and Prevention (CDC). Among African Americans, the rate is even higher. Homicide is the leading cause of death in this age group, ahead of vehicle accidents, suicide, and all diseases. "The single greatest cause of death for young black men between the ages of 18 and 35 is homicide. And that's crazy. That is crazy,"[14] says former president Barack Obama.

> "The single greatest cause of death for young black men between the ages of 18 and 35 is homicide. And that's crazy. That is crazy."[14]
>
> —Barack Obama, former president of the United States

Disparities by Race

In part because of gang and other criminal violence in urban areas, the gun homicide rate for African Americans is higher than for other races. The 2016 gun homicide rate for African Americans was 19.8 per 100,000 people. That is five times higher than the rate for Hispanics (4.0 per 100,000) and twelve times higher than for non-Hispanic whites (1.7 per 100,000).

The racial disparities in gun homicide rates vary widely by state. For example, an African American living in Wisconsin is twenty-six times more likely to be fatally shot than a white person in that state, according to researchers at Boston University. By contrast, an African American in Arizona is 3.2 times more likely than a white person to be killed by a gun. Researchers at Boston Uni-

> "Racial disparities in advantage translate into racial disparities in firearm violence victimization."[15]
>
> —Molly Pahn, Anita Knopov, and Michael Siegel, researchers at Boston University

versity believe that differences in economic and social advantage contribute to the differences in gun death rates. The researchers explain:

> These differences across states occur primarily because the gap between levels of disadvantage among white and black Americans differs sharply by state. For example, Wisconsin—the state with the highest disparity between black and white firearm homicide rates—has the second-highest gap of any state between black and white incarceration rates, and the second-highest gap between black and white unemployment rates. Racial disparities in advantage translate into racial disparities in firearm violence victimization.[15]

Homicide, including gang-related homicide, is the leading cause of death for African Americans aged fifteen to twenty-four.

Categories of Homicides

According to the CDC, there were 14,415 firearm homicides in the United States in 2016. The circumstances around each death were as distinct as the individuals who lost their lives. Nevertheless, for the purpose of organizing efforts to reduce these deaths, the CDC categorizes these deaths by the circumstances leading up to the shootings. This risk-based analysis helps public health officials know where to focus their resources.

The largest single category of gun homicides is shootings related to criminal activities. All murders are criminal activities, of course, but this category is reserved for shootings that occur in connection with another crime, such as armed robbery, burglary, the drug trade, rape and sexual assault, and motor vehicle theft. A 2018 study by the CDC found that 37.4 percent of all homicides were precipitated by another crime. More than half of these homicides—56.4 percent—occurred while the crime was in progress.

The murder of Wintez Ta'Vorius Moody, a twenty-two-year-old man in Covington, Georgia, was one such homicide. On November 5, 2018, Moody called 911 just after 9:00 p.m. to report a burglary in progress at his home. When Newton County deputies arrived, they found Moody inside, dead of multiple gunshot wounds. Two days later, a US Marshals task force and Newton County sheriff's investigators arrested twenty-year-old Trae Johnson as a suspect in the killing. Johnson faces felony murder and armed robbery charges.

Interpersonal Conflicts

The second-largest category of homicides is violence that arises from interpersonal relationships. These conflicts are the cause of 35.9 percent of all homicides, according to the 2018 CDC study. The chance of being killed due to interpersonal conflicts is much higher for women than for men. Nearly 70 percent of female gun homicides are the result of interpersonal conflicts, according to the 2018 CDC report. Nearly half of female homicides (47.6 percent) are related to intimate partner violence. Another 5.8 percent are the result of jealousy or a lover's triangle. Slightly more than 8 percent of female homicides are the result of family conflicts, 4.4 percent grow out of interpersonal violence within the previous month, and 3.5 percent are the result of nonintimate relationship problems.

Michelle Lane of Advance, North Carolina, is one of the thousands of women who were the victims of interpersonal gun

---

A Fight Between Brothers Turns Deadly

The CDC reports that about 7 percent of homicides arise from conflicts between family members. An argument between two brothers led to a firearm death in Lexington, Kentucky, on November 15, 2018. Shortly after 9:00 a.m., police responded to a call about a shooting. When they arrived they found twenty-eight-year-old Jaymes Coffey with a gunshot wound. Witnesses said Jaymes had been arguing with his younger brother, twenty-six-year-old Timothy Coffey. As the argument intensified, Timothy produced a handgun and shot his older brother. He then fled in a vehicle. Jaymes was pronounced dead at the scene. Police later found Timothy on a nearby street and took him into custody. He was charged with murder.

Jaymes's friends remember him as outgoing, well liked, and funny. "It's going to take a while for a lot of us to get over [this]. Just his energy being in the room, and just his presence and what that offered," says Jacob Collins, a friend. Collins said Jaymes, who was also known as Jordy, had tried to help his younger brother overcome some mental and behavioral issues. "I didn't know his brother particularly well, but I do know that Jordy loved him very much," says Collins. "It's one of the just most shocking, unsettling things, because Jordy made such an effort to bring him out and introduce him to people and include him in things."

The incident was the twenty-second homicide of the year in Lexington. All but three of the murders were committed with guns.

Quoted in Garrett Wymer, "Man Charged with Brother's Murder Appears in Court," WKYT, November 16, 2018. www.wkyt.com.

violence in 2018. She had lived in fear of her husband, Joel, for years. In 2012 Joel pointed a gun at her and threatened suicide. Things got worse in 2018. Joel and Michelle separated, and in September, Joel, a former marine who served from 1990 to 1994, was hospitalized for depression, suicidal thoughts, and post-traumatic stress disorder. On September 25, he told Michelle, "I would love no more than to hurt you."[16] The next day Michelle filed for a domestic violence protective order, stating that she feared imminent, serious bodily injury. The order was granted on October 2. It informed Joel that he would be arrested if he visited Michelle's home. It also barred him from possessing, receiving, or purchasing a firearm. The court order did no good. On November 2, 2018, Michelle was at home with the four-year-old

Nearly 70 percent of female gun homicides are the result of interpersonal conflicts. Nearly half of female homicides are related to intimate partner violence.

child that she and Joel had together, as well as her sixteen-year-old daughter from a previous relationship, when Joel showed up with a handgun. An argument broke out and gunshots were fired. Michelle's sixteen-year-old daughter ran to a neighbor's house for assistance. The four-year-old was still inside the home as the shooting continued. When police arrived, they found Michelle and Joel inside, both with gunshot wounds but alive. The Lanes were taken to a nearby hospital and underwent surgery. The children were unharmed and were placed in the care of social services for eventual placement with other family members.

Men are also the victims of shootings arising from interpersonal conflicts. According to the CDC, 23.8 percent of male homicides are the result of interpersonal conflicts. This includes 8.8 percent related to intimate partner violence, 1.9 percent resulting from a lover's triangle, 1.2 percent growing out of interpersonal violence within the previous month, 5.9 percent resulting from nonintimate relationship problems, and 6 percent resulting from family conflicts.

Mass Shootings

While many shootings—and the majority of shootings of women—involve people who know each other well and even live together, some shootings are committed by people who decide to open fire on complete strangers in public settings. When these shootings result in the deaths of three or more people, they are known as mass shootings. According to a study by University of Alabama criminal justice professor Adam Lankford, the United States had 31 percent of the world's mass shooters, even though it makes up just 4.6 percent of the world's population. According to Lankford's count, the United States was home to 90 of the world's 202 mass shooters from 1966 to 2012.

Critics of Lankford's work point out that it is impossible to know how many mass shootings occurred in the forty-six-year time span his study covers, since officials in remote parts of the world did not keep count of such incidents. In addition, Lankford excludes gang-related shootings, drive-by shootings, hostage-taking incidents, robberies, and acts of terrorism. For example, Lankford excludes the 2008 attack in Mumbai, India, that claimed 168 lives.

A 2018 study by John R. Lott Jr., president of the Crime Prevention Research Center, comes to a very different conclusion than Lankford's study does. Lott finds that the United States had less than 1.43 percent of the world's mass public shooters

Parents of a Mass Shooting Victim Speak Out

Around 11:20 p.m. on November 7, 2018, Ian David Long, a twenty-eight-year-old Marine Corps combat veteran, arrived at the Borderline Bar & Grill in Thousand Oaks, California, a popular country-western night spot where people gathered to dance and have a good time. It was College Country Night at the bar, and 150 to 200 mostly young patrons were inside. But Long was not there to listen to music and socialize. He was there to kill. Dressed in black and armed with a .45 caliber Glock 21 semiautomatic pistol, Long threw a smoke bomb into the entrance and swept in behind, gunning down eleven patrons and employees, aged eighteen to forty-eight. Ventura County sheriff's deputy Ron Helus responded to the emergency call in less than three minutes and engaged the shooter. Long shot and killed the officer and then took his own life.

In a cruel twist of fate, one of Long's victims, twenty-seven-year-old Telemachus "Tel" Orfanos, had survived the mass shooting in Las Vegas a year before, only to be slain at the Borderline Bar & Grill. The fact that their son was present at two mass shootings magnifies the problem of gun violence for Tel's parents. "When you have 300 million guns in private hands, more guns than you have in places like Yemen or Syria, there is something seriously wrong," says Tel's father, Marc Orfanos. Tel's mother, Susan Schmidt-Orfanos, is calling for stricter gun laws. "I hope to God no one sends me anymore prayers. I want gun control. No more guns!" she says.

Quoted in Vanessa Romo and Dina Kesbeh, "'This Is Going to Be Absolutely Heart-Wrenching': The Thousand Oaks Shooting Victims," NPR, November 8, 2018. www.npr.org.

from 1998 to 2012. Lott counts the same number of American shooters as Lankford does but adds more than twelve hundred mass shooters in other countries, mainly by including terrorist attacks recorded in the University of Maryland's Global Terrorism Database. For example, by including terrorist attacks, the number of mass shootings in the Philippines increases from 11 to 120. "We find at least *fifteen times* more mass public shooters than Lankford in less than a third the number of years,"[17] says Lott.

Whether the United States has 31 percent of the world's mass shooters or less than 2 percent, it still has a higher rate of mass shooting deaths than most advanced countries, even when including terrorist killings. Lott's study finds that for the fourteen-year period from 1998 to 2012, the number of mass shooting deaths per 100,000 people is 0.11 in the United States. This rate is about three times higher than Germany's (0.04), four times higher than France's (0.03), six times higher than the United Kingdom's (0.02), ten times higher than Canada's (0.01), and twelve times higher than Italy's (0.009). Only Norway, with a rate of 1.4 mass shooting deaths per 100,000 people; Finland with a rate of 0.4; and Russia with a rate of 0.15 exceed the mass shooting death rate in the United States among advanced nations.

According to the *Washington Post*, which keeps a running tally of mass shootings on a web page devoted to the topic, there have been 158 mass shootings in the United States since 1966, claiming 1,135 lives. In the fifty years before 1966, there were only twenty-five public mass shootings in which four or more people were killed, according to author and criminologist Grant Duwe. The number of mass shootings and the number of victims have risen dramatically in recent years, with the five deadliest US mass shootings occurring since 2007. These include the 2017 shooting at the Route 91 Harvest music festival in Las Vegas, Nevada, that left 58 people dead and 851 wounded,

> "A student's obituary should not contain the phrase 'Gunned down while studying for a chemistry test.'"[18]
>
> —Kathy Durham, a social studies teacher at West Wendover High School in West Wendover, Nevada

and the 2016 attack at the Pulse nightclub in Orlando, Florida, that killed 49 and injured 50. Mass shootings make headlines not only because of the large number of deaths but also because of the senselessness of being murdered by a total stranger.

Mass shootings are also especially heartbreaking because they often involve a disproportionate number of young people. The 2018 mass shootings at Marjory Stoneman Douglas High School in Parkland, Florida, and Santa Fe High School in Santa Fe, Texas, took the lives of twenty-two teens and five adults. The 2012 slaughter at Sandy Hook Elementary School in Newtown, Connecticut, claimed the lives of twenty children, ages six and seven, and six adults. The 2007 rampage at Virginia Polytechnic Institute and State University in Blacksburg,

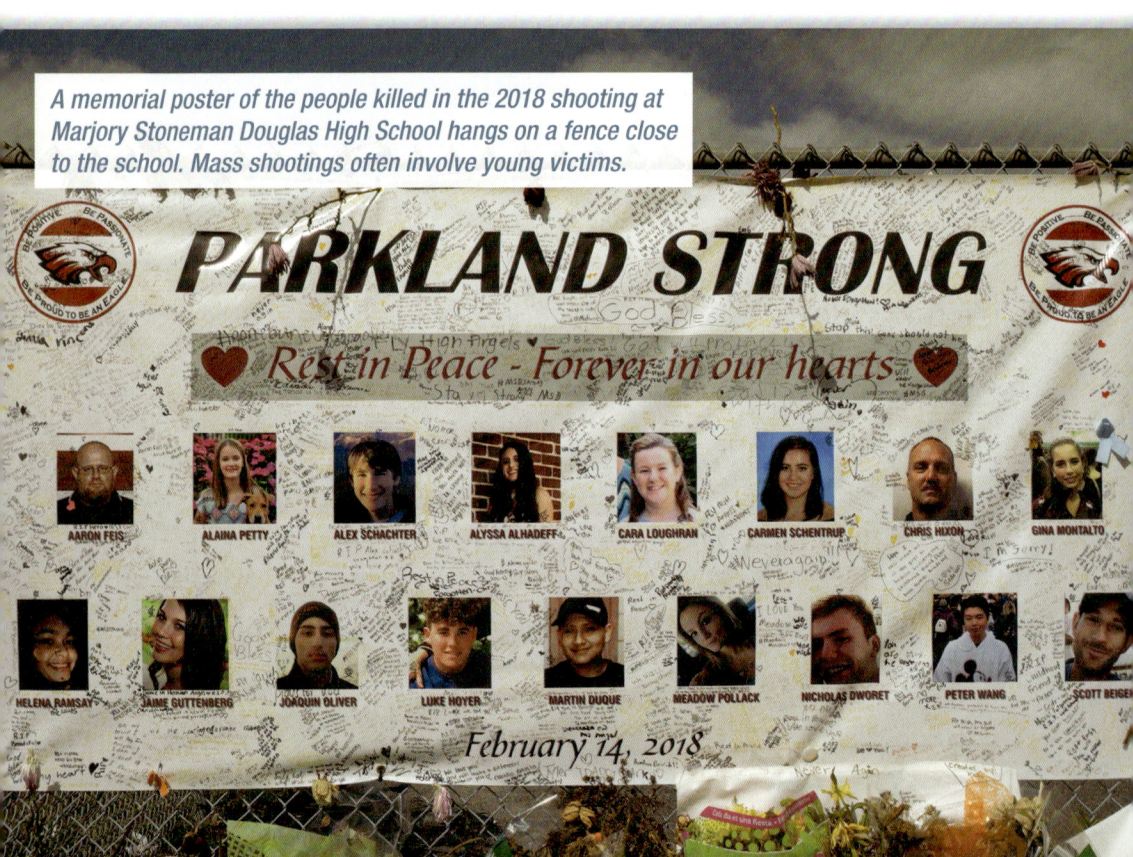

A memorial poster of the people killed in the 2018 shooting at Marjory Stoneman Douglas High School hangs on a fence close to the school. Mass shootings often involve young victims.

Virginia, killed twenty-five college students under age twenty-eight, including seven teens. "A student's obituary should not contain the phrase 'Gunned down while studying for a chemistry test,'"[18] writes Kathy Durham, a social studies teacher at West Wendover High School in West Wendover, Nevada.

Everyday Gun Violence

While horrifying, mass shootings are not the biggest gun violence problem the United States faces. Mass shootings make up less than 1 percent of all gun-related homicides. The biggest problem is the ongoing, day-to-day killings. Gun violence researchers Molly Pahn, Anita Knopov, and Michael Siegel write:

> The first step in treating the epidemic of firearm violence is declaring that the everyday gun violence that is devastating the nation is unacceptable. Mass shootings and terrorist attacks should not be the only incidents of violence that awaken Americans to the threats to our freedom and spur politicians to action. . . . As public health scholars who study firearm violence, we believe that our country is unique in its acceptance of gun violence. Although death by firearms in America is a public health crisis, it is a crisis that legislators accept as a societal norm.[19]

If the United States is going to make progress in reducing gun violence, the public must understand that its most serious problem is the daily death toll, which rarely makes headlines.

CHAPTER THREE

Guns and Suicide

Thirteen-year-old Cayman Naib of Newton Square, Pennsylvania, was a typical teenager. "He loved to play video games. He loved to play soccer. He was full of life," says his father, Farid Naib. "Life was about as good as it could be." However, on March 4, 2015, Cayman received an email from his school telling him he was failing a course. He was upset by the bad news. "He went, he found this gun, which I had no idea that he knew where it was," Farid recalls. The gun was locked with a trigger guard, which remained locked. Nevertheless, Cayman somehow found a way to discharge the gun and take his own life. "I bought the gun thirty years ago for personal protection," Farid explains. "When the kids were born, I should have thrown it away. I didn't throw it away. I went out and bought a trigger guard for it, locked it and then forgot about it. I thought I'd done everything I needed to do, and I was totally wrong."[20]

Only thirty minutes had passed from the time Cayman received the email until he took his life. His father is convinced that if there were no gun in the house, the crisis would have passed, and Cayman would be alive today. "Kids get upset," says Farid. "And they make bad decisions when they're upset. And by having a gun in house that they can access, you give them the ability to make that bad decision permanent."[21]

Research supports Farid Naib's conclusion. According to the Brady Center to Prevent Gun Violence, 71 percent of people who attempt suicide do so within an hour after making the decision. If they do not succeed, the vast majority do not go on to take their own lives. According to the Harvard T.H. Chan School of Public

Health, 93 percent of those who attempt suicide and survive do not end up dying by suicide at a later date. Seventy percent never attempt suicide again. "A gun in the home makes it too easy for someone to find a permanent and tragic solution to a temporary feeling,"[22] says Dan Gross, president of the Brady Center to Prevent Gun Violence.

> "A gun in the home makes it too easy for someone to find a permanent and tragic solution to a temporary feeling."[22]
>
> —Dan Gross, president of the Brady Center to Prevent Gun Violence

A Surge in Suicides

Suicide has been on the rise in the United States in recent years. In 2009 suicide surpassed traffic accidents to become the second-leading cause of nondisease death in the United States. That was only the beginning. In 2017 the number of suicides surged to its highest level in thirty years. In 2017 a total of 47,173 Americans took their own lives. From 1999 through 2017, the suicide rate increased 33 percent, from 10.5 to 14.0 per 100,000 people, according to a 2018 report by the CDC. Suicide is now the second-leading cause of death of people ages ten to twenty-four, behind only accidental death, which includes falls, poisonings, and drug overdoses. "It's really stunning to see such a large increase in suicide rates affecting virtually every age group,"[23] says Katherine Hempstead of the Robert Wood Johnson Foundation, a public health organization.

Guns were used in 51 percent of all US suicides in 2016, the most recent year for which data is available, accounting for 22,938 self-inflicted deaths. The number of firearm suicides dwarfs all other kinds of firearm deaths in the United States, including homicides (14,415), law enforcement use and legal self-protection (510), and accidents (496). "Much of our discussion about gun violence in the United States and what to do about it does not recognize that for every homicide with a firearm, there are two suicides with a firearm, and, importantly, as public health officials,

Research shows that 71 percent of people who attempt suicide do so within an hour of making the decision. Having a gun in the home makes it easier for a person to end their life due to temporary feelings of hopelessness.

we recognize that these are preventable deaths,"[24] says Daniel W. Webster, director of the Center for Gun Policy and Research at Johns Hopkins University.

An Effective Means of Suicide

The grim fact is that firearms are an effective means of taking one's life. According to a study by the American Association of Suicidology, only one in twenty-five suicide attempts ends in death. Among young people aged fifteen to twenty-four, only one in one hundred attempts ends in death. These statistics refer to all suicide attempts regardless of method. The odds of a fatal result rise dramatically when firearms are used. A report by the Brady Center to Prevent Gun Violence found that 91 percent of firearm suicide attempts end in death. This is because firearm "injuries are instantaneous and leave little time for medical intervention or for the victim to reconsider their decision,"[25] says the Brady Center to Prevent Gun Violence.

This was certainly the case in the 2016 suicide of eighteen-year-old Brandy Vela of Texas City, Texas. Vela had been bullied and harassed for weeks by an ex-boyfriend and his new girlfriend. The two were later charged under Texas law with setting up fake online dating profiles for Brandy. These fake profiles offered sex and included Brandy's phone number. The dating profiles resulted in countless disturbing phone calls. "Sometimes, she wouldn't sleep," Brandy's father, Raul Vela, recalls. "She'd call me at night. She'd say, 'Dad, I can't sleep. My phone keeps ringing.'"[26] The teen changed her phone number several times, but the bullying continued. "The harsh messages and fake social media pages created to bully and impersonate her became too much for her to handle,"[27] the family later wrote online.

On the day of her suicide, Brandy sent a text to her older sister, Jacqueline, saying, "I love you so much just remember that please and I'm so sorry for everything."[28] Fearing that Brandy might harm herself, Jacqueline notified their parents and rushed home. "I was the first one here," Jacqueline says. "I ran upstairs and I looked in her room and she's against the wall and she has a gun pointed at her chest and she's just crying and crying and I'm like, 'Brandy please don't, Brandy no.'"[29] Brandy's parents arrived and begged the teen not to take her life. "We tried to persuade her to put the gun down but she was determined," says Raul. "She said she'd come too far to turn back."[30] Moments later, Brandy pulled the trigger. "I was in my parents' room and I just heard the shot and my dad just yelled, 'Help me, help me, help me,'"[31] Jacqueline remembers. Brandy was rushed to a local hospital, but she did not survive.

Gun Availability and Suicide

In Brandy Vela's instance, as in the case of Cayman Naib, the gun used in the suicide belonged to another family member. This is the case in the overwhelming majority of teen firearm suicides. According to a study by the Brady Center to Prevent Gun Violence, 82 percent of teen firearm suicides involve a family member's gun. According to an earlier study by researchers at the University of Colorado–Denver, the mere presence of a gun in a home affects how adolescents think about suicide. The researchers found that adolescents with a suicide plan were seven times more likely to include a gun in the plan if their household had a gun, compared to adolescents in households without a gun. "Typically, people utilize what is most available to them,"[32] says John Draper, director of the National Suicide Prevention Lifeline.

The presence of a gun in the home is a major factor in all suicides, according to a 2016 study by researchers at Boston University School of Public Health in Massachusetts. They found that

The presence of a gun in the home is a major factor in many suicides. Studies show that adolescents with a suicide plan were seven times more likely to include a gun in the plan if their household had a gun.

US states with high gun ownership rates also had high gun suicide rates. For example, Wyoming, Montana, and Idaho were ranked first, second, and third in gun ownership rates, with household gun ownership rates of 72.8 percent, 68.4 percent, and 61.6 percent, respectively. These states also ranked first, second, and third in male gun suicide rates, with 26.1, 23.5, and 21.0 gun suicides per 100,000 people. The three states also ranked high for female gun suicides, although females generally are less likely to use guns to commit suicide. "We found a strong relationship between state-level firearm ownership and firearm suicide rates among both genders," write the researchers. "State-level firearm ownership was associated with an increase in both male and female firearm-related suicide rates and with a decrease in nonfirearm-related suicide rates."[33]

> "State-level firearm ownership was associated with an increase in both male and female firearm-related suicide rates and with a decrease in nonfirearm-related suicide rates."[33]
>
> —Michael Siegel and Emily F. Rothman, researchers at the Department of Community Health Sciences, Boston University School of Public Health

Differences in Gender

Gun availability is not the only factor in firearm suicides. If it were, then it would follow that the use of guns in suicides would be uniform across genders and ages. However, that is not the case. The Boston University study found that 41 percent of all US households have guns. But while guns are more or less equally available to men and women in those households, suicidal men use them far more frequently than suicidal women do. According to the CDC, 57 percent of male suicides involved guns, compared to just 32 percent of female suicides.

Men also take their own lives at a much higher rate than women do. According to the CDC's 2018 National Vital Statistics Report, 77 percent of the nation's suicides are men. Because more men take their own lives than women do, and because they use

> "It's when other risk factors are coupled with firearm ownership that the excess risk is formed."[35]
>
> —Daniel W. Webster, director of the Center for Gun Policy and Research at Johns Hopkins University

firearms more often, the overwhelming majority of firearm suicides involve men. The CDC's report states that 19,647 of the nation's 22,938 firearm suicides—86 percent—involved men. The Boston University study found that the nationwide gun suicide rate for men is about seven times higher than it is for women—14.2 per 100,000 for men compared to 2.1 per 100,000 for women.

Any public health initiative to reduce incidents of disease and death must address the issue of who is most at risk. In the case of firearm suicides, it is men. "The gendered nature of firearm violence across causes highlights the need for targeted forms of intervention that address cultural components of firearm use by and against men,"[34] write the authors of the University of Washington's 2018 study of firearm deaths around the world.

The disparity between genders in firearm suicide points to a problem with studies that look at only one factor, such as gun availability. Webster observes:

> People in public health and people who study epidemiology and risk as it relates to firearms mostly think about it in terms of a relative risk: the more guns, the more deaths there are with respect to homicides and suicides in particular. But I think what's lost in that, however, is absolute risk. In the United States, for example, roughly one in three homes will have at least one firearm, and the vast majority of those homes with firearms, nothing bad will happen. It's when other risk factors are coupled with firearm ownership that the excess risk is formed.[35]

Other factors that can lead to gun violence include anger, mental health problems, and substance abuse.

> ## A Man with Dementia Takes His Life
>
> In the United States 9 percent of Americans sixty-five and older are diagnosed with dementia, a disease marked by mental decline and personality changes. Many of these people own guns, creating a danger to themselves and those around them.
>
> One such person was seventy-five-year-old Bill Collins, a retired heavy-equipment operator and army veteran. Collins owned nine guns, including a .22 caliber pistol that he kept in his pocket at all times. He usually loaded his pistol with rat shot, small lead pellets for killing snakes and vermin.
>
> On June 14, 2015, Collins grew upset, believing someone had stolen things from his room. He raised his hand to strike his daughter, fifty-year-old Christal Collins. Her fiancé, Allen Holtzman, intervened. Bill pulled the .22 pistol from his pocket and shot Allen in the chest, knocking him down. Fortunately, the gun was loaded with rat shot, and Allen survived. "Wrong damn shells!" Bill said after shooting, realizing what had happened.
>
> With Bill still firing, Christal dragged Allen to her bedroom and called 911. While on the phone, she heard her father slam the door to his bedroom. After a short pause, she heard another loud sound. Bill had reloaded his pistol with bullets and shot himself in the head. Christal says she wishes she had removed all the guns from the house, but she adds, "I honestly don't know if we could have taken them away."
>
> Quoted in JoNel Aleccia and Melissa Bailey, "Unlocked and Loaded: Families Confront Dementia and Guns," *USA Today*, July 1, 2018. www.usatoday.com.

Breakdown by Race

Just as firearm suicide rates are not uniform across gender, neither are they uniform across race. According to the CDC, non-Hispanic whites are the only group in which the percentage of firearm suicides exceeds the group's share of the population. According to the US Census Bureau, non-Hispanic whites make up 60.7 percent of the US population, but they account for 86 percent of all firearm suicides. By contrast, Hispanic or Latino Americans make up 18.1 percent of the US population but less than 6 percent of firearm suicides. Non-Hispanic African Americans make up 13.4 percent of the US population but less than 6 percent of firearm suicides. Asians or Pacific Islanders make up 6 percent of the population but only 1.5 percent of firearm suicides. Native Americans make up 1.3 percent of the US population but less than 1 percent of firearm suicides. While every life lost to firearm suicide matters, from a public health perspective, non-Hispanic whites are at the greatest risk of firearm suicide.

Part of the reason for the high firearm suicide rate among whites is that they also make up a disproportionate share of suicides overall. According to the CDC, non-Hispanic whites made up 34,727 of the nation's 44,965 suicides in 2016, or 81 percent of the total. When it comes to firearm suicides, white men make up 85.5 percent of the male firearm suicides, and white women make up an astounding 88 percent of the female firearm suicides. In fact, white women make up just 33 percent more of the female

Firearm suicide rates are not uniform across race or gender. While non-Hispanic whites make up 60 percent of the US population, they account for 86 percent of all firearm suicides.

> ### Reducing Firearm Suicides
>
> Daniel W. Webster is the director of the Center for Gun Policy and Research at Johns Hopkins University. In 2018 he provided editorial commentary for a JAMA Network video about firearm mortality. Here he discusses reducing firearm suicides.
>
>> There are other strategies that may be very specific and unique to suicide reduction that we have not fully examined and invested in. One thing that many people in public health are beginning to talk about is ways to change a culture, in essence, about holding firearms from individuals when they're going through some crisis that might elevate their risk for suicide. So just as a friend or family member, as a caring thing to do about someone's safety, would say, "let me get you, let me drive you home because you've had too much to drink," you do the same thing with saying, "Let me hold your guns while you're going through this divorce. Let me keep your guns after you just lost your job and are very distraught.
>>
>> We also talk about this as what physicians can do in their role in counseling patients and their families to reduce access to firearms to lower suicide risk. But, in my opinion, it's a much bigger public health challenge to really change a culture about firearm access and suicide. It is the thing that is leading to the greatest number of firearm deaths in our country. Whenever we've had big breakthroughs in public health, it's always been a combination of policy and cultural change.
>
> Quoted in Elena Guobyte et al., "Global Mortality from Firearms, 1990–2016," YouTube, August 28, 2018. https://youtu.be/VucFxSkbDwY.

US population than all other races combined, but they account for seven times the number of female firearm suicides—2,888 compared to just 400.

An Increasing Risk by Age

The number of firearm suicides also varies by age group. Unlike other nondisease causes of death, such as drug overdoses or homicides, the risk of firearm suicide increases with age. The mortality rate of other nondisease causes of death tends to peak in the ten-year age group of twenty-five to thirty-four and then taper off in the older age groups. For example, there were 4,510 firearm homicides in the twenty-five to thirty-four age group in 2016 but 2,555 in the forty-five to fifty-six age group and 1,420 in the fifty-five to sixty-four age group. Firearm suicides follow the opposite trend, ramping up by age. There were 3,298 firearm suicides in the twenty-five to thirty-four age group in 2016 but 3,873 in the forty-five to fifty-six age group and 4,067 in the fifty-five to sixty-four age group.

The rates of firearm suicides per 100,000 people are even more startling. In 2016 the rate of firearm suicides was 16.49 per 100,000 in the twenty-five to thirty-four age group, 18.74 in the forty-five to fifty-six age group, and 18.98 in the age group eighty-five and older—the highest rate of any age group. "Who knew that firearm violence was increasingly an old white guy problem?"[36] says Garen Wintemute, an emergency physician and director of the Violence Prevention Research Program at UC Davis School of Medicine.

> "Who knew that firearm violence was increasingly an old white guy problem?"[36]
>
> —Garen Wintemute, an emergency physician and director of the Violence Prevention Research Program at UC Davis School of Medicine

The research suggests that for almost three-quarters of those who attempt suicide, the crisis passes and never recurs. In such cases securing or temporarily removing firearms from the home would likely save thousands of lives a year. Since such a change would not be permanent, it would not threaten gun rights in any meaningful way. The difficulty is in identifying those who are suicidal and then having a simple program for gun owners to follow.

CHAPTER FOUR

The Human Toll of Gun Violence

Statistics shape public health policy. Public health officials use numbers to decide where to put money, resources, and intervention for maximum benefit. However, statistics do not tell the whole story of an emerging public health issue. Behind each gun violence statistic is a human being who has been injured or killed. The mental trauma that accompanies a death or injury can last a lifetime both for those who survived being wounded and for those who lost loved ones. Each person's story is different, but each one helps illuminate the problem of gun violence. "Numbers can numb," says David Studdert, a professor of medicine and law at Stanford University. "I think they are a useful starting point, but it doesn't really get us down to the micro level where the problems exist and the solutions are to be found."[37]

Kidnapped, Raped, and Shot

Sara Cusimano was just starting eighth grade when she experienced terror and trauma that few people will ever go through or understand. In a 2017 interview, she talked with a reporter about the ongoing pain and fear that resulted from a day that began like any other. On August 18, 1994, Cusimano was sitting in the front seat of her mother's SUV at a Time Saver convenience store near Louis Armstrong New Orleans International Airport in Kenner, Louisiana. It had been an exciting day for Sara—the first day of eighth grade. As her mother paid for the gas, Cusimano leaned back in her seat and closed her eyes. Then she heard the driver's side door open. She opened her eyes and saw a man armed with a handgun get into the car. Cusimano recalls not being frightened at that point. "I didn't really realize the gravity of what was happening, until he started to pull away," she says. "I remember looking down to the passenger's side and seeing the lock. That was the moment when I realized that he was going to kill me."[38]

The kidnapper, Billy Pittman, drove onto Interstate 10 heading west but then crossed the median and headed east. He exited and drove to the end of a road near the airport. He grabbed Cusimano by the hands and led her into an overgrown field. "I was begging for any opportunity to get away, and then trying to bargain, I guess, for ways for him to let me go, to convince him to let me go," she says. Pittman made her lie down on a piece of cardboard. There, he raped her. Throughout the assault, Pittman held the gun to Cusimano's head. "I fought, and I fought, and I

Statistics do not show the mental trauma behind each act of gun violence. The stress and anguish suffered by victims can last a lifetime.

fought," Cusimano recalls. At one point she got her hand onto the gun. "I thought about shooting him for that, you know, point two seconds that I had my hand on the gun. I thought about shooting him. I imagined what would happen after that, if I was able to shoot him, and I couldn't bring myself [to do it]." After raping her, Pittman told Cusimano to kneel, close her eyes, and count to ten. "I remember feeling almost a sense of relief. It was over. It was done. He was going to run away. I remember getting to 'three,' then he shot me." The bullet entered Cusimano's forehead but shattered before it could enter her brain. A large fragment exited the backside of her neck. "I remember feeling like I had been hit with a sledgehammer. I honestly thought maybe he had punched me."[39]

Cusimano is haunted by memories of the attack. "There are days when I haven't worked hard enough to push the memories to the back of my head, and I feel the burn down my face and out the back of my neck," she says. Every detail remains clear in her mind. "You never forget," she says. Cusimano says that the first few months after the shooting were all about her physical recovery, and that distracted her from mental and emotional issues. But that condition was temporary. "People think that if you are a gunshot survivor, and you survive, that's the end to the journey. They think you walk out that hospital door, and that's it. And it's just so far from the truth."[40] Cusimano points out that she is a multiple trauma survivor—kidnapping, rape, and gunshot. But she says the gunshot trauma is the worst:

> "If he had just not pulled that trigger, my life would be so different, so different. That millisecond decision that he made destroyed the entire rest of my life."[41]
>
> —Sara Cusimano, gunshot survivor

> Out of all of that, if he had just not pulled that trigger, my life would be so different, so different. That millisecond decision that he made destroyed the entire rest of my life. The sounds that I hear at night, the being scared of a car

backfiring in a parking lot. Taking the garbage can to the street at night, after it's dark, terrifies me. And it's all just because he chose to pull the trigger. Nobody makes those connections between what the real impact is to that decision. I mean, it's a second, a millisecond. The decision that you're making is to torture somebody every day for the rest of their life.[41]

Pittman pleaded not guilty by reason of insanity to attempted first-degree murder, aggravated rape, second-degree kidnapping, and carjacking, but he was held mentally competent to stand trial. He was convicted on all counts and sentenced to 160 years' imprisonment. Pittman's decision to pull the trigger affected not only Cusimano but all of those around her. "I have a mother and a father and brothers and sisters and aunts and uncles and cousins and friends, and every single one was impacted,"[42] she says.

Caught in the Crossfire

The entire family of six-year-old Emely Ramirez was affected by her shooting as well. On October 12, 2018, Emely's mother, Brenda Ramirez, was standing outside her car with her daughters, ages thirteen and seventeen, at a gas station in Los Angeles when a BMW pulled up beside her car. A Pontiac was parked on the other side of her car. Emely was buckled into her car seat in between. Without warning, the people inside the BMW and Pontiac began shooting at each other. Brenda screamed at her older daughters to get onto the ground as she scrambled to get Emely out of the crossfire. Bullets tore through the car's metal and shattered its glass as Brenda struggled to unbuckle Emely's safety straps. When Brenda finally managed to pull Emely to safety, she found that her daughter's back was wet with blood. Emely had been hit by a bullet. "Mommy I'm tired, I want to go to sleep,"[43] Emely said as the shooters drove off.

Traumatized by a School Shooting

Melissa Falkowski was teaching a journalism class at Marjory Stoneman Douglas High School on February 14, 2018, when nineteen-year-old Nikolas Cruz went on a shooting rampage at the school. She describes some of her feelings that day and in the weeks that followed.

> When the fire alarm went off, I was with my fourth-period newspaper class. I told them, "Let's go." But in the hallway, a security person sent us back into the classroom—she said it was a code red. The kids gathered in a corner, like they'd been taught. I moved them into a storage closet when I saw on my phone that shots had been fired. . . .
>
> It wasn't until I got home later that I heard the number: 17. I cried on my front porch, and that night I slept less than two hours—I couldn't quiet my mind. For a few days, I walked around numb, not eating much. I couldn't be alone or not doing something, so I threw myself into media interviews. I felt like it was my responsibility to keep people talking about what happened. I had planned to go to six funerals, but I ended up going to only three because I just couldn't handle it. . . .
>
> I worry that once things slow down, I'll break down in moments of quiet. I've already been through phases where I was numb and in shock, then totally upset and crying, then angry. There are so many emotions. You don't know which one you're going to get at any given time.

Quoted in Elizabeth Van Brocklin, "The Wounds You Can't See: Four Women on the Lasting Trauma of Gun Violence," The Trace, May 22, 2018. www.thetrace.org.

Emely survived, but she has a bullet lodged in her back. She, her mother, and her sisters are haunted by what happened that evening. Emely has returned to school but is prone to throwing fits and demanding that her mother buy her things. Emely's older sisters are troubled as well. The eldest wants to sleep in her mother's bed, and the thirteen-year-old has trouble sleeping. "They say, 'I'm OK,' but I know they're not,"[44] Brenda says.

Brenda is troubled as well. "I never feel fear. I always say, 'Well, everything's gonna be good, and we're gonna fix it and everything's gonna be right,'" Brenda says. "At that moment, I feel like nothing was good and nothing was right. And I don't know why it was happening to me." She felt completely unprepared for what happened. "If there's an earthquake I have my gallons of water here, in my car," she says. "Wherever I go, I have alcohol, bandages. . . . I always prepare for everything. I wasn't prepared for this. Nobody told me how to act." She is angry at the selfishness of the shooters, their utter disregard for innocent bystanders. "They saw there were kids . . . and they didn't care," says Brenda. "They just care about their anger or whatever it was in their heads, the evil things."[45]

Lasting Trauma

The trauma of gun violence extends beyond the families of the people who are killed or wounded and affects their communities. "Every time a person gets shot, especially a young person, there are literally hundreds of people who are affected by that shooting,"[46] says Brad Stolbach, the clinical director of Healing Hurt People-Chicago, a trauma treatment organization. Those people, Stolbach adds, often are not thought about in discussions about gun violence.

> "Every time a person gets shot, especially a young person, there are literally hundreds of people who are affected by that shooting."[46]
> —Brad Stolbach, the clinical director of Healing Hurt People-Chicago

Kimberly Greer is one of them. A drug counselor at St. Bernard Hospital in Chicago, Illinois, Greer has had her life turned upside down by gun violence on three separate occasions. In 2006 her eighteen-year-old daughter, Ryann, was in the front seat of a friend's car when an assailant opened fire. Ryann's friend was killed. Ryann was struck in the head by a bullet but survived. Greer spent years helping her daughter regain her motor skills through at-home rehabilitation.

In the wake of the Parkland, Florida, shooting in 2018, protesters of gun violence hold signs. The trauma of gun violence often extends beyond the loved ones of victims and can impact an entire community.

No sooner was Ryann on her way to recovery when Greer's thirty-year-old son, Ricky, was shot on the steps of his home as he was leaving for his job at a US post office in March 2012. He did not survive. "I feel bad for every mother who has lost a child," says Greer. "I don't think you ever get through grieving. You learn to live with it." For Greer, living with it means going to work every day. "I don't have a choice to take off [from work] and grieve," she says. "Because if I stay home and grieve, after a while I'm not going to have a home to grieve at."[47]

While doing her best to cope with her son's death and her daughter's injury, Greer suffered another blow. In June 2016 her eighteen-year-old nephew, Jordan "BayBay" Liggins, was murdered while sitting in a car. Every day on her way to work, Greer drives past the spot where her nephew was shot. "I have to suck up my grief. Whatever I'm feeling I gotta suck it up and keep it moving," she says. "Go to work because you can't fall to pieces." Greer has trouble sleeping, often waking to thoughts of her daughter, son, and nephew. "I'm traumatized,"[48] she says.

A New, More Wary Normal

Such emotional trauma will remain with the survivors, says Susan Johnson, director of Chicago Survivors, an organization that works with families who have lost a loved one in a shooting. "It will continue to be a loss for them for the rest of their lives," says Johnson. "Others around them will want them to return to their normal selves, and they're going to have to find a new normal self."[49]

For Jeffrey Shine, his "new normal self" is a person more suspicious of strangers on the street and less able to do the things he loves, including running and dancing. "The experience has been traumatic," he says. "Because, I was a guy that was running,

Gunshot survivors and families of gunshot victims need to learn new coping skills to deal with the trauma. Counseling services can often be hard to obtain, especially in urban centers.

dancing, five or six records in a row. I'm still dancing—no running!—but I'm not dancing as much. I will probably never get one hundred percent, but I am grateful to be alive, because I could have been dead."[50] In 2015 Shine, a retired Chicago postal worker, was heading home, carrying a bag of groceries, when two young men approached. Brandishing a gun, they demanded his money and valuables. As Shine reached in his pocket to give them the money, one of the robbers shot him in the knee. As Shine collapsed, the men grabbed two gold chains from his neck and fled. Shine says the emotional wound was greater than the physical pain:

> "It will continue to be a loss for them for the rest of their lives. Others around them will want them to return to their normal selves, and they're going to have to find a new normal self."[49]
>
> —Susan Johnson, director of Chicago Survivors

> The initial shot itself, that didn't hurt. Just being robbed period was devastating—especially coming from where I came from. I've seen robberies before, I've seen people shot at, I've seen people shot. But for it to happen to me was just kind of unbelievable. I'm like, "Really? Why'd you have to shoot me? I gave you what you wanted. You want my money *and* my life?" It felt terrible. . . . It hurt not just in the sense of getting shot, but it hurt my feelings, being hurt by another individual that's just like me.[51]

Shine says he is now much more alert on the street. "I call it 'my antenna is up,'" he says. If he sees strangers on the street, especially young men, he tries to figure out what their intentions are before he encounters them. This wariness is a big change, one that Shine regrets. "I always thought, 'You do your thing, that's fine, that's what you do. I do my thing, that's what I do.' But people just won't let you live and be happy."[52]

More Help Is Needed

Jaleel Abdul-Adil, the codirector of Chicago's Urban Youth Trauma Center, believes that not enough research has been devoted to the effects of gun violence on gunshot survivors, families, and the community. "I don't think we truly understand the complexity of what it's like to survive on a day-to-day basis in under resourced, historically oppressed and dangerously impoverished communities,"[53] says Abdul-Adil.

Gunshot survivors and the families of gunshot victims need to learn new coping skills to deal with the trauma, but counseling can be hard to obtain, especially in urban centers. For example, Chicago has six hospitals that are designated as trauma and mental health treatment centers dealing with issues that stem from violence, and there are another four hundred clinics and agencies that offer mental health services. However, these facilities do not have enough staff trained in handling gunshot trauma to accommodate all of those seeking help. As a result, the waiting lists are full. "There's nowhere where you can call and get in tomorrow,"[54] says Alexa James, executive director of National Alliance on Mental Illness Chicago.

Without counseling, survivors of gun violence may show signs of what Reverend Carol Reese, a chaplain with the Department of Trauma at Stroger Hospital in Chicago and a violence prevention expert, calls moral injury. Often experienced by war veterans, moral injury is a person's belief that he or she is no longer capable of acting in a fair or ethical way. As a result, some of these traumatized individuals may be drawn into more gun violence. Each shooting multiplies the number of people experiencing mental and emotional trauma, which in turn feeds the epidemic of gun violence.

The amount of gun violence in the United States is so great that only the most horrific shootings shoulder their way past political debates, celebrity news, and sports scores to enter the American consciousness. But each gun death and each

> ### A Childhood Shooting Accident Changes a Life
>
> Benedict Jones is proud that he can live on his own despite being paralyzed from the chest down as a result of a childhood shooting accident. Still, he sometimes wonders about the course his life has taken. In a 2017 interview, he reflects on what happened to him and what might have been.
>
> Shooting was a hobby that Jones shared with his father. In 1991, at the age of eleven, Jones brought out all of his father's guns for a game of cops and robbers with a friend. Jones thought all of them were unloaded. One was not. That was the one the friend happened to pick up. He shot Jones in the throat. The bullet shattered a bone in his spinal column, and bone fragments went into his spinal cord, causing paralysis from the chest down. Jones reflects on his life since that day.
>
>> Being able to overcome the daily life of living in a chair, the daily burdens that confront you, most of the time gives me this wellspring of confidence that I can do anything. And I don't know how true that is. Because beyond this, it takes an order of magnitude higher to achieve those great successes that we all dream of. And I put a lot on myself in terms of vision for what I want to achieve in the world, a contribution that I want to make that would be significant to the world. And sometimes I feel like, "Have I been cheated of that opportunity?"
>
> Quoted in Erin Calabrese, "Journey of a Bullet," NBC News, June 20, 2017. www.nbcnews.com.

gun injury leaves a deep, psychic scar on the survivors and the community—something that does not often make the news and is rarely discussed. "There's a line that I as an American crime reporter have come across a lot in news releases: the injuries were not considered life threatening," says reporter Amber Hunt. "After twenty years of reporting about violent crime, I have come to hate those words. They are too simplistic, too dismissive. Yeah, a life didn't end, but there's a decent chance it changed forever. Isn't that newsworthy, too?"[55]

CHAPTER FIVE

What Is Being Done to Reduce Gun Violence?

Gun violence covers several kinds of violence, each with its own causes and each requiring a separate approach to address it. A crackdown on crime will not affect suicide rates. Strategies to reduce suicide will not decrease homicides. Addressing those problems will not greatly affect domestic violence. Currently, policy makers rely on gun retailers to prevent some potentially dangerous people from obtaining guns. But many gun transactions take place outside the retail system through private sales, gifts, and even the black market in stolen guns. With the prevalence of gun violence in the United States, new strategies are being developed to save lives.

Research

Effective public health policy begins with a thorough understanding of a problem. Such understanding often begins with research, but research into firearms as a public health issue has been hampered by public policy. The Dickey Amendment, adopted by Congress in 1996, states that funds made available for injury prevention and control at the CDC cannot be used to advocate or promote gun control. Although this was meant to prevent advocacy-based research, the actual effect was to prevent federal funding for any gun violence research. "Congress over the last 2 decades has placed limits on that science from being conducted," write the editors of *JAMA*. "This attempt to suppress research into gun violence resulted in a 64% decline in the number of firearm studies . . . between 1998 and 2012."[56]

In the wake of the shooting at Sandy Hook Elementary School in 2012, President Barack Obama ordered the National Institutes of Health (NIH) to sponsor research on gun violence and how to prevent it. The initiative funded fourteen firearm-related studies for $11.4 million in three years. Funding for those studies was not renewed in 2017 under President Donald Trump and the Republican-controlled Congress. Critics believe this change signals a lack of interest in understanding and preventing gun violence. However, NIH officials said they would continue research on gun violence through other means. "We haven't stopped funding work in this area and we intend on continuing to fund work in this area,"[57] says Lawrence Tabak, the NIH's principal deputy director.

> "Congress over the last 2 decades has placed limits on [gun violence research] from being conducted. This attempt to suppress research into gun violence resulted in a 64% decline in the number of firearm studies . . . between 1998 and 2012."[56]
>
> —Editorial board of *JAMA*

Research is one way for policy makers to decide which initiatives for reducing gun violence are working and which are not. These initiatives include tightening background checks, raising gun ownership age limits, requiring the use of gun locks, and restricting the sales of semiautomatic weapons.

Background Checks

Background checks are designed to decrease gun violence by keeping guns out of the hands of people most likely to use them on themselves or others. This includes people with a history of mental illness or a criminal record. Many gun rights advocates support background checks because they focus on shooters, not guns, as the problem. "It seems to be common for a lot of these shootings, in fact almost all of the shootings, is the mental state of the people," said Senator Chuck Grassley of Iowa, a gun rights supporter, after the shooting at Marjory Stoneman Douglas High

After the Sandy Hook Elementary School shooting in 2012, President Barack Obama ordered the National Institutes of Health to sponsor research on gun violence and prevention.

School in 2018. "We have not done a very good job of making sure that people that have mental reasons for not being able to handle a gun getting their name into the FBI files, and we need to concentrate on that."[58]

The FBI currently processes about 20 million background checks every year, using the NICS. However, not everyone who purchases a firearm passes a background check. That is because federal law only requires licensed sellers to run background checks. Private sellers, such as an individual gun owner who decides to sell a firearm, are not required to perform a background check.

Many states have passed tougher gun laws. Ten states and the District of Columbia require private gun sellers to perform background checks before selling a firearm. Maryland and Pennsylvania require background checks for the private sales of handguns but not of rifles. Eight other states close the loophole by restricting all gun sales—public and private—to people who have first obtained a gun license, a process that includes passing a background check. This removes the burden of running the background check from the gun sellers while achieving the same result. Thirty states do not require background checks. Many gun control advocates believe that requiring background checks for all sales is one way of reducing gun violence. "As part of a comprehensive gun violence prevention strategy, we must require a criminal background check for every gun sale, and ensure that all relevant records are in the background check system,"[59] states Everytown for Gun Safety, a nonprofit organization that advocates for gun violence prevention.

> "We have not done a very good job of making sure that people that have mental reasons for not being able to handle a gun getting their name into the FBI files, and we need to concentrate on that."[58]
>
> —Chuck Grassley, US senator from Iowa

Age Limits

Some policy experts see raising the gun owner age limit as a way to decrease both homicides and suicides. Federal law currently prohibits licensed dealers from selling a handgun to any person under age twenty-one, but the federal age limit drops to eighteen if the gun is purchased from a private seller. Federal law also prohibits the possession of a handgun by any person under age eighteen, but there is no federal minimum age for the possession of rifles.

As in the case of background checks, many states have passed tougher age limit restrictions for gun ownership. Gun safety advocates point out that men aged eighteen to twenty have a higher violent crime rate than other age groups. In addition, many people in that age group lack the impulse control to be a responsible gun owner. Fifteen states have made twenty-one the minimum age for purchasing any handgun, even for private sales. After the shooting at Marjory Stoneman Douglas High School, the Florida legislature raised the age for purchasing rifles from eighteen to twenty-one. In doing so, Florida joined Hawaii and Illinois as the only states that ban the sale of all types of guns to people under twenty-one.

Research at the University of Washington–Seattle suggests that raising the age limit for gun ownership could reduce firearm suicides. The researchers interviewed 153 adolescents and young adults who survived an almost lethal suicide attempt. Twenty-four percent of the subjects reported that less than five minutes elapsed from the time when they decided to end their life and when they attempted suicide. This extreme impulsiveness suggests that raising the age limit for gun sales to twenty-one could save lives.

Gun Locks

Because of the impulsive nature of many teen and young adult suicides, the researchers at the University of Washington concluded that safe storage, including the use of trigger locks, may also decrease suicides. They write, "Investigators have observed a lower suicide risk in households where safe storage practices exist than in those where firearms are stored unlocked or loaded."[60]

> "Investigators have observed a lower suicide risk in households where safe storage practices exist than in those where firearms are stored unlocked or loaded."[60]
>
> —Joseph A. Simonetti et al., researchers at the University of Washington

Gun locks can also reduce accidental deaths. The US Government Accountability Office estimates that 31 percent of accidental firearm deaths could be prevented by the use of childproof safety locks or loading indicators, devices that show whether a firearm has a round of ammunition in its chamber.

In 2005 Congress passed and President George W. Bush signed into law the Protection of Lawful Commerce in Arms Act. The act requires gun dealers, importers, and manufacturers to provide a gun storage or safety device for any handgun sold or transferred in the United States, with exceptions for law enforcement and other government agencies. Like federal background checks, the law does not apply to transfers of

Because of the impulsive nature of teenagers, researchers have concluded that safe storage measures and trigger locks can decrease the number of suicides among young people.

guns by private sellers. More importantly, it does not require that gun owners use the devices.

As with age limits and background checks, individual states have enacted tougher gun storage laws. Massachusetts requires that all firearms be stored in a locked container or equipped with a tamper-resistant mechanical lock or other safety device. California, Connecticut, and New York require such devices only when the gun owner lives with a person who is not allowed by federal law to possess a gun, such as a convicted felon. The Connecticut law applies only to guns that are loaded. These are the only four states that require gun owners to use gun locks.

Steps to Prevent Gun Violence

The *Journal of the American Medical Association* (*JAMA*) is a peer-reviewed medical journal published by the American Medical Association. After the 2017 mass shooting in Las Vegas, the editors of *JAMA* wrote about what can be done to reduce gun violence:

> The shooting in Las Vegas, Nevada, that left 59 people dead, 10 times that number wounded, and thousands of people with the psychological distress from being present at the scene during and after the massacre has once again raised the issue of what we as a nation can and should do about guns. The solution lies in not just focusing on Las Vegas and the hundreds of other mass shootings that have occurred in the United States in the last 14 months, but rather to underscore that on average almost 100 people die each day in the United States from gun violence. . . .
>
> As with any epidemic, prevention is important. Physicians and others should ask about guns in the home, especially for high-risk patients, and advise about removal and safe storage. Good evidence has shown that safe storage of firearms is effective in reducing misuse. . . .
>
> Guns kill people. More background checks; more hotel, school, and venue security; more restrictions on the number and types of guns that individuals can own; and development of "smart guns" may help decrease firearm violence. But the key to reducing firearm deaths in the United States is to understand and reduce exposure to the cause, just like in any epidemic, and in this case that is guns.

Howard Bauchner et al., "Death by Gun Violence—a Public Health Crisis," *Journal of the American Medical Association*, November 14, 2017. https://jamanetwork.com.

Some states require gun locks to be included in both dealer sales and private sales. California requires that all guns sold in the state, even rifles, include an approved gun safety device. Massachusetts requires the devices to be included in all sales of handguns and semiautomatic rifles. Unlike federal law, the

Massachusetts law applies to dealers who sell semiautomatic rifles. Connecticut and New Jersey require gun locks for sales of handguns. No other states require gun locks to be included in private sales.

By requiring locks for all guns, Massachusetts is the only state that prevents minors from accessing firearms. According to the Giffords Law Center to Prevent Gun Violence, the Massachusetts law is effective in preventing teen suicide. The center reports that guns are used in just 9 percent of youth suicides in Massachusetts, compared to 39 percent of youth suicides nationwide. In addition, the overall suicide death rate among Massachusetts youth is 35 percent lower than national average.

High-Tech Sensors

Standard gun locks are mechanical in nature, requiring a key or combination to unlock them. Many gun owners do not like such devices because they delay the use of a gun in an emergency, when seconds count. To overcome this problem, some gun manufacturers are using high technology to secure the weapons while making them immediately available for use in an emergency.

Shotgun manufacturer O.F. Mossberg & Sons has created a technology that pairs electronics in a ring that is worn on the finger with electronics in a gun to lock and unlock the weapon. Without the ring nearby, the gun will not shoot. When the ring is nearby, the gun's embedded sensor recognizes the radio signal from the ring and unlocks the gun. This is more convenient than a standard trigger lock, because the user does not have to find the key to manually unlock the gun. It also prevents anyone—even people in the household—from using the gun without the ring. Since many suicides, especially teen suicides, are committed using guns that belong to other family members, this technology has the potential to reduce firearm suicides. It also has the potential to reduce the number of accidental firearm deaths, since the secured guns will not fire without the electronic signal.

Electronic gun locks could have a large impact not only on accidental deaths and suicides but also on the criminal use of guns. As the University of Pittsburgh study of guns recovered at crime scenes shows, about 80 percent of guns used to commit crimes do not belong to the perpetrator, but instead belonged to someone else. Many of these guns were stolen. If all guns were outfitted with electronic locks that can only be opened with a remote device, like the O.F. Mossberg & Sons ring, or with a biometric scanner, like the ones used in cell phones and laptop computers, stolen guns would become useless. Such electronic gun locks could be engineered to render the gun permanently inoperable if the locks are tampered with in any way.

Banning Semiautomatic Weapons

Federal law already bans fully automatic weapons, known as machine guns, which allow the user to fire many rounds with one pull of the trigger. Many people believe that semiautomatic weapons, which require the user to pull the trigger to fire each round but automatically load the next round, should also be banned. For support, gun control advocates often point to the effects of Australia's National Firearms Agreement of 1996. Enacted after a lone gunman armed with two semiautomatic rifles shot and killed thirty-five people and injured eighteen others in Port Arthur, Tasmania, the Australian law banned the sale of certain semiautomatic rifles and shotguns. It also required people who owned the banned weapons to turn them in to the government. In exchange, the government paid the owners for the assessed value of the weapons they surrendered. Under the buyback plan, the Australian government collected more than 650,000 guns at the cost of 500 million Australian dollars. Richard Franklin, an associate professor at James Cook University in Australia, credits the law with steep declines in firearm deaths. "In Australia we went from 614 firearm deaths in 1990 to 274 in 2016. That's a fall from 3.4 deaths per 100,000 people to 1 per 100,000 in 2016," he

Semiautomatic guns are on display at a gun shop. Many people believe that these types of guns, which automatically load a bullet after each one is fired, should be banned.

says. "We've seen a decline particularly in firearm suicides and an absence of mass shootings."[61]

The Australian ban came two years after United States banned the sale of semiautomatic weapons as part of the 1994 Public Safety and Recreational Firearms Use Protection Act. However, the American ban allowed the owners of 1.5 million semiautomatic weapons to keep them. The US law also exempted 650 weapons deemed suitable for target practice, hunting, and other sporting purposes. In part because of these exemptions, and in part because semiautomatic weapons were only used in 2 percent of gun crimes before the ban, the United States did not experience the steep decline in firearm deaths

> ## Firepower Matters
>
> When President Ronald Reagan was shot by a would-be assassin in 1981, he survived being wounded by a .22 caliber bullet that broke a rib, punctured a lung, and caused internal bleeding. Reagan recovered quickly, but the outcome might have been different if the would-be assassin had used a larger-caliber handgun, according to a 2018 study published in *JAMA Network Open*.
>
> Anthony Braga of Northeastern University and Philip Cook of Duke University analyzed data on 221 gun homicides and 1,012 nonfatal shootings that occurred in Boston. Only one of the shootings involved a rifle; the rest involved handguns. The researchers divided guns used in the shootings into three categories: small, medium, and large. Small included .22, .25, and .32 caliber handguns; medium included 380s, .38s, and 9mms; and large included .40s, .44 magnums, .45s, 10mms, and 7.62 x 39s.
>
> The researchers found that a person shot with a medium-caliber weapon was roughly 2.3 times more likely to die than someone shot with a small-caliber gun. Someone shot with a large-caliber gun was 4.5 times more likely to die than someone shot with a small-caliber gun. "The implication," write the researchers, "is that if the medium- and large-caliber guns had been replaced with small caliber (assuming everything else unchanged) the result would have been a 39.5% reduction in gun homicides." The study suggests that regulating and reducing the firepower of handguns could substantially reduce firearm fatalities without affecting the ownership of rifles and small- or even medium-size handguns.
>
> Quoted in Christopher Ingraham, "Actually, Guns Do Kill People, According to a New Study," *Washington Post*, July 27, 2018. www.washingtonpost.com.

that Australia did. As a result, Congress did not renew the ban when it expired in 2004.

In the wake of the Las Vegas and Parkland mass shootings, many gun control advocates have called for a new assault weapons ban. Representative David N. Cicilline of Rhode Island and Senator Dianne Feinstein of California have proposed a new assault weapons ban. Both bills (one in the House and one in the

Senate) borrow language and definitions from the expired law, although the list of banned guns has been updated to include newer weapons. The proposed ban faces an uphill political battle. Such a law would not only have to pass the House, it would need fifty-one votes to pass in the Senate. Forty-three US states currently allow the sale and possession of assault weapons, and it would only take forty-one Senate votes to stall the bill.

Seven states have taken action against assault weapons. Three states—California, Connecticut, and New Jersey—had already passed assault weapons bans before the federal law was enacted in 1994. Another four states—Hawaii, Maryland, Massachusetts, and New York—passed their own bans before the federal law expired in 2004.

With the passage of an outright ban of semiautomatic weapons unlikely, gun control advocates have focused on one feature of the weapons that makes them most deadly: the size of the magazine that holds the rounds that can be fired without reloading. Eight states have outlawed high-capacity magazines, which allow ten or more shots to be fired without reloading. Following the shootings at the Las Vegas strip and in Parkland, Florida, members of Congress introduced a bill that outlaws large-capacity ammunition feeding devices that accept more than ten rounds of ammunition. Since high-capacity magazines are not needed for sport purposes, some supporters of gun rights are open to limiting their capacity.

> "There is no magic gun evaporation fairy. There is no path to get the United States of America to a guns-per-capita ratio on par with other countries."[62]
>
> —BJ Campbell, a political analyst

No Single Solution

There is no single solution for ending gun violence. "There is no magic gun evaporation fairy," writes political analyst BJ Campbell. "There is no path to get the United States of America to a guns-per-capita ratio on par with other countries. It is not remotely feasible."[62]

The best public health officials can hope for is a piecemeal approach designed to draw support from both gun owners and gun control advocates. This approach can include limiting automatic weapon magazine size, requiring gun locks, raising gun ownership age limits, and tightening background checks. These steps will not end the gun violence epidemic overnight, but they could combine to reduce homicides, suicides, and accidental firearm deaths.

SOURCE NOTES

Introduction: A Deadly Epidemic

1. Quoted in Gun Violence Memorial, "Pamela Crumpton Hooks, Age 34," May 18, 2018. http://gunmemorial.org.
2. Quoted in Gun Violence Memorial, "Pamela Crumpton Hooks, Age 34."
3. Quoted in Gun Violence Memorial, "Pamela Crumpton Hooks, Age 34."
4. Quoted in Stanford Health Policy, "Gun Violence and Suicide by Firearm Is a Public Health Epidemic," March 16, 2017. https://healthpolicy.fsi.stanford.edu.

Chapter One: The Making of a Crisis

5. Quoted in Nurith Aizenman, "Gun Violence: How the U.S. Compares with Other Countries," *Goats and Soda* (blog), NPR, October 6, 2017. www.npr.org.
6. Quoted in Elena Guobyte et al., "Global Mortality from Firearms, 1990–2016," YouTube, August 28, 2018. https://youtube.com/VucFxSkbDwY.
7. Quoted in John Lott, "The Media Plays Dishonest Numbers Game with Guns," *Hill*, June 24, 2017. https://thehill.com.
8. David French, "What Critics Don't Understand About Gun Culture," *Atlantic*, February 27, 2018. www.theatlantic.com.
9. Charles M. Blow, "America Is the Gun," *New York Times*, February 25, 2018. www.nytimes.com.
10. Anthony Fabio, interview with the author, November 28, 2018.
11. Quoted in Jeff Stein, "The NRA Is a Powerful Political Force—but Not Because of Its Money," Vox, October 5, 2017. www.vox.com.

Chapter Two: When Gun Violence Becomes Commonplace

12. Quoted in Courtney Carpenter, "'A Big Talker, but He Wasn't a Gangster': Family of Murdered Teen Warns About Social Media Personas," CW39 Houston, November 19, 2018. https://cw39.com.
13. Quoted in Carpenter, "'A Big Talker, but He Wasn't a Gangster.'"
14. Quoted in Alex Berezow, "African-American Homicide Rate Nearly Quadruple the National Average," American Council on Science and Health, August 10, 2017. www.acsh.org.
15. Molly Pahn et al., "Gun Violence in the US Kills More Black People and Urban Dwellers," Conversation, November 8, 2017. https://theconversation.com.
16. Quote in Michael Hennessey, "Domestic Violence Protection Order Fails When Mother and Father Found Shot in Davie County," Fox 8, November 2, 2018. https://myfox8.com.
17. Quoted in Glenn Kessler, "Does the U.S. Lead the World in Mass Shootings?," *Washington Post*, September 5, 2018. www.washingtonpost.com.
18. Kathy Durham, "Opinion: A Student's Obituary Should Never Say 'Gunned Down While Studying for Chemistry,'" PBS, February 16, 2018. www.pbs.org.
19. Pahn et al., "Gun Violence in the US Kills More Black People and Urban Dwellers."

Chapter Three: Guns and Suicide

20. Farid Naib, "Cayman's Story," YouTube, September 8, 2015. https://youtu.be/taUfarsaZYo.
21. Naib, "Cayman's Story."
22. Quoted in Brady Campaign to Prevent Gun Violence, "The Truth About Suicide and Guns," September 8, 2015. www.bradycampaign.org.

23. Quoted in Sabrina Tavernise, "U.S. Suicide Rate Surges to a 30-Year High," *New York Times*, April 22, 2016. www.nytimes.com.
24. Quoted in Guobyte et al., "Global Mortality from Firearms, 1990–2016."
25. Brady Campaign to Prevent Gun Violence, "The Truth About Suicide and Guns."
26. Quoted in Rucks Russell, "Family, Friends of Cyber-bullying Victim Want Justice," KHOU 11, December 1, 2016. www.khou.com.
27. Quoted in Christopher Brennan, "Ex-boyfriend Arrested for Sharing Nude Photos of Texas Teen Who Killed Self After Cyberbullying," *New York Daily News*, March 16, 2017. www.nydailynews.com.
28. Quoted in Lucy Pasha-Robinson, "Teenager Killed Herself in Front of Parents After 'Relentless' Cyber Bullying," *Independent* (London), December 2, 2016. www.independent.co.uk.
29. Quoted in Pasha-Robinson, "Teenager Killed Herself in Front of Parents After 'Relentless' Cyber Bullying."
30. Quoted in Russell, "Family, Friends of Cyber-Bullying Victim Want Justice."
31. Quoted in Pasha-Robinson, "Teenager Killed Herself in Front of Parents After 'Relentless' Cyber Bullying."
32. Quoted in Dan Roe, "Why Aren't We Talking About Suicide When We Talk About Gun Violence?," *Self*, April 13, 2018. www.self.com.
33. Michael Siegel and Emily F. Rothman, "Firearm Ownership and Suicide Rates Among US Men and Women, 1981–2013," *American Journal of Public Health*, July 2016. www.ncbi.nlm.nih.gov.
34. Global Burden of Disease 2016 Injury Collaborators, "Global Mortality from Firearms, 1990–2016," *Journal of the American Medical Association*, August 28, 2018. https://jamanetwork.com.

35. Quoted in Guobyte et al., "Global Mortality from Firearms, 1990–2016."
36. Quoted in Stanford Health Policy, "Gun Violence and Suicide by Firearm Is a Public Health Epidemic."

Chapter Four: The Human Toll of Gun Violence

37. Quoted in Stanford University, "Gun Violence and Racial Justice," YouTube, March 13, 2017. https://youtu.be/tBli9vHZ61U.
38. Quoted in Erin Calabrese, "Journey of a Bullet," NBC News, June 20, 2017. www.nbcnews.com
39. Quoted in Calabrese, "Journey of a Bullet."
40. Quoted in Calabrese, "Journey of a Bullet."
41. Quoted in Calabrese, "Journey of a Bullet."
42. Quoted in Calabrese, "Journey of a Bullet."
43. Quoted in Sonali Kohli, "A 6-Year-Old Got Shot in an Apparent Gang Fight. Here's What Her Mother Wants You to Know," *Los Angeles Times*, October 31, 2018. www.latimes.com.
44. Quoted in Kohli, "A 6-Year-Old Got Shot in an Apparent Gang Fight. Here's What Her Mother Wants You to Know."
45. Quoted in Kohli, "A 6-Year-Old Got Shot in an Apparent Gang Fight. Here's What Her Mother Wants You to Know."
46. Quoted in Ryan Connelly Holmes, "Chicago's Gun Violence Crisis Is Also a Mental Health Crisis," *PBS NewsHour*, August 22, 2017. www.pbs.org.
47. Quoted in Holmes, "Chicago's Gun Violence Crisis Is Also a Mental Health Crisis."
48. Quoted in Holmes, "Chicago's Gun Violence Crisis Is Also a Mental Health Crisis."
49. Quoted in Holmes, "Chicago's Gun Violence Crisis Is Also a Mental Health Crisis."
50. Quoted in Calabrese, "Journey of a Bullet."
51. Quoted in Calabrese, "Journey of a Bullet."
52. Quoted in Calabrese, "Journey of a Bullet."
53. Quoted in Holmes, "Chicago's Gun Violence Crisis Is Also a Mental Health Crisis."

54. Quoted in Holmes, "Chicago's Gun Violence Crisis Is Also a Mental Health Crisis."
55. Amber Hunt, "Aftermath Podcast: The 48-Year-Old Wound," Cincinnati.com, May 22, 2018. www.cincinnati.com.

Chapter Five: What Is Being Done to Reduce Gun Violence?

56. Howard Bauchner et al., "Death by Gun Violence—a Public Health Crisis," *Journal of the American Medical Association*, November 14, 2017. https://jamanetwork.com.
57. Quoted in Meredith Wadman, "NIH Emails Reveal Divisions over Renewal of Gun Research Program," *Science*, October 18, 2017. www.sciencemag.org.
58. Quoted in Ashley Killough et al., "Amid Continued String of Mass Shootings, Gun Control Going Nowhere in Congress," CNN, February 15, 2018. https://edition.cnn.com.
59. Everytown for Gun Safety, "Background Checks on All Gun Sales," 2018. https://everytown.org.
60. Joseph A. Simonetti et al., "Psychiatric Comorbidity, Suicidality, and In-Home Firearm Access Among a Nationally Representative Sample of Adolescents," *JAMA Psychiatry*, February 2015. https://jamanetwork.com.
61. Quoted in James Cook University, "Tough Laws Prevent Gun Deaths, Global Report Finds," ScienceDaily, October 19, 2018. www.sciencedaily.com.
62. BJ Campbell, "The Magic Gun Evaporation Fairy," Handwaving Freakoutery, March 31, 2018. https://medium.com.

ORGANIZATIONS AND WEBSITES

American Public Health Association
800 Eye St. NW
Washington, DC 20001
www.apha.org

A nonprofit organization, the American Public Health Association speaks out on public health issues and policies. The gun violence area of its website provides articles, fact sheets, research and data, news, useful links, and other resources.

Brady Campaign to Prevent Gun Violence
840 First St. NE, Suite 400
Washington, DC 20002
www.bradycampaign.org

Founded in 1974 as the National Council to Control Handguns, the Brady Campaign to Prevent Gun Violence was renamed in 2001 in honor of James Brady and his wife, Sarah. The organization has a goal of cutting the number of US gun deaths in half by 2025 through stronger background checks, cracking down on irresponsible gun dealers, and educating the public about gun violence.

Coalition to Stop Gun Violence (CSGV)
805 Fifteenth St. NW
Washington, DC 20005
www.csgv.org

The CSGV is a nonprofit organization founded in 1974 with the goal of building communities free from gun violence. The organization pursues this goal through research, policy development, and lobbying for gun control legislation.

Everytown for Gun Safety

450 Lexington Ave.
New York, NY 10022
www.everytown.org

Founded in 2014 by former New York City mayor Michael Bloomberg, Everytown for Gun Safety is a nonprofit organization that advocates for gun control and against gun violence. With a membership surpassing 4 million, it has successfully lobbied for gun control legislation at the local and state levels.

Giffords Law Center to Prevent Gun Violence

268 Bush St., Suite 555
San Francisco, CA 94104
http://lawcenter.giffords.org

A nonprofit organization with a mission to save lives from gun violence, the center provides a wealth of legal information on areas such as the Second Amendment, background checks, guns in public, gun owner responsibilities, and more. Its website features information about the laws of each state as well as federal laws.

GunPolicy.Org

www.gunpolicy.org

This website presents research from the University of Sydney in Australia. It features an interactive chart maker that allows the user to compare gun death rates per one hundred thousand people for any mix of countries and instantly see a bar graph illustrating the comparisons.

Gun Violence Archive

1718 M St. NW
Washington, DC 20036
www.gunviolencearchive.org

This not-for-profit organization provides free online public access to accurate information about gun-related violence in the United

States. Its home page keeps a list of gun-related incidents for the year, updated hourly. The list includes number of incidents, deaths, injuries, children and teens killed or injured, home invasions, and more.

Marshall Project
156 W. Fifty-Sixth St., Suite 701
New York, NY 10019
www.themarshallproject.org

The Marshall Project is a nonpartisan, nonprofit news organization that seeks to create and sustain a sense of national urgency about the US criminal justice system. Its website includes a mass shooting page that links to dozens of web pages with information on mass shootings and gun control.

National Rifle Association (NRA)
11250 Waples Mill Rd.
Fairfax, VA 22030
https://home.nra.org

Founded in 1871, the NRA is a nonprofit organization that advocates for Second Amendment rights. The organization has about 5 million members and lobbies for and against gun legislation.

The Trace
www.thetrace.org

The Trace is a nonprofit newsroom covering gun violence in America. Its website includes a daily roundup of news stories on gun violence and gun control legislation. It features an interactive map plotting the locations of nearly forty thousand incidents of gun violence nationwide.

FOR FURTHER RESEARCH

Books

John Allen, *Thinking Critically: Gun Control*. San Diego: ReferencePoint, 2018.

Anne Cunningham, *Guns: Conceal and Carry*. New York: Greenhaven, 2018.

Adam Furgang, *Everything You Need to Know About Gun Violence*. New York: Rosen, 2018.

Carol Hand, *Gun Control and the Second Amendment*. Minneapolis: Essential Library, 2017.

Bridget Heing, *Investigating Mass Shootings in the United States*. New York: Rosen, 2018.

Bradley Steffens, *Gun Violence and Mass Shootings*. San Diego: ReferencePoint, 2019.

Internet Sources

Mark Abadi, "The 12 Deadliest Mass Shootings in Modern US History," Business Insider, February 15, 2018. www.businessinsider.com.

BBC, "America's Gun Culture in 10 Charts," March 21, 2018. www.bbc.com.

Bonnie Berkowitz et al., "Mass Shooting Statistics," *Washington Post*, March 14, 2018. www.washingtonpost.com.

Erin Calabrese, "Journey of a Bullet," NBC News, June 20, 2017. www.nbcnews.com.

John Woodrow Cox, "Inside an Accused School Shooter's Mind: A Plot to Kill '50 or 60. If I Get Lucky Maybe 150,'" *Washington Post*, March 3, 2018. www.washingtonpost.com.

Editorial staff of *Eagle Eye*, "Our Manifesto to Fix America's Gun Laws," *Guardian* (Manchester), March 23, 2018. www.theguardian.com.

Rachel Ehrenberg, "What We Do and Don't Know About How to Prevent Gun Violence," *Science News*, March 9, 2018. www.sciencenews.org.

David French, "What Critics Don't Understand About Gun Culture," *Atlantic*, February 27, 2018. www.theatlantic.com.

German Lopez, "America's Unique Gun Violence Problem, Explained in 17 Maps and Charts," *Vox*, April 4, 2018. www.vox.com.

INDEX

Note: Boldface page numbers indicate illustrations.

Abdul-Adil, Jaleel, 50
accidental deaths, 56, 59
Advance, North Carolina, 23–25
African Americans
    firearm suicide rate, 37–38
    gun deaths of men ages eighteen to thirty-five, 20
    homicide rate, 20
    mental health of males, after being shot, 14
age
    nondisease deaths and, 39–40
    purchase or use of guns and, 12, 55–56
American Association of Suicidology, 32
Asians, firearm suicide rate, 38
assault weapons, 60–63, **61**
Australia, 60–61
automatic weapons, 60

background checks, 13, 17, 53–55
Baous, Melissa, 4
Blacksburg, Virginia, 28–29
Blow, Charles M., 12
Boston University, 20–21, 34–35, 36
Brady Center to Prevent Gun Violence, 30, 32–33, 34
Brady Handgun Violence Prevention Act (1993), 12
Braga, Anthony, 62
Brazil, 8
Bullard, Dmitri, 4
bullying, 33
Bush, George W., 56

California
    assault weapons bans, 62–63
    gun homicides and ownership rates, 17
    trigger lock law, 57, 58
Campbell, BJ, 63

Canada
    gun deaths in, 8, 14
    gun ownership in, 13–14
    mass shootings in, 27
    number of guns in, 9
Centers for Disease Control and Prevention (CDC)
    gender and homicides from interpersonal conflicts, 22–23, 25
    gun deaths
        during criminal activity, 22
        1999–2017, **6**
        of young people ages fifteen to twenty-four, 20
    research funds and, 52
    suicides using guns
        gender and, 35–36
        race and, 37, 38–39
        rate, 31
Chicago, Illinois, 4, 50
Cicilline, David N., 62–63
Coffey, Jaymes (Jordy), 23
Coffey, Timothy, 23
Cofield, D.Z., 19
Collins, Bill, 37
Collins, Christal, 37
Collins, Jacob, 23
Congress
    assault weapons ban bills proposed, 62–63
    high-capacity magazine ban bill, 63
    research funds and, 52–53
    role in bicameral system of, 16–18
Connecticut, 57, 63
Covington, Georgia, 22
criminal activity
    deaths during, 6, 22
    high-tech sensors and stolen guns, 60
    history of, and purchase of guns, 11–12
    homicides related to gang violence, 19–20
    injuries from, 48–49

most guns used during, are obtained illegally, 16
Cruz, Nikolas, 45
Cusimano, Sara, 41–44

Dallas Gun Show, **13**
Dardar, Tonia, 4
deaths
  accidental, 56, 59
  of African American men ages eighteen to thirty-five, 20
  in Australia, 60–61
  in Canada, 8, 14
  at church services, 17
  during criminal activity, 6, 22
  grief of families, 47–48
  increase in, 14
  mass shootings
    during church services, 17
    at entertainment venues, 26, 27–28, 58
    at schools, 4, **28,** 28–29, 45, 53
  May 18–19, 2018, 4–5
  1999–2017, **6**
  related to gang violence, 19–20
  relationship between number of guns and, 8
  risk of nondisease, and age, 39–40
  suicide as second-leading nondisease cause, 31
  in workplaces, 7
  of young people ages fifteen to twenty-four, 20
  of young people seventeen years old and younger, 7
  See also suicides
dementia, 37
Dickey Amendment (1996), 52
District of Columbia, 54
Draper, John, 34
Drutman, Lee, 18
Durham, Kathy, 29
Duwe, Grant, 27

effects
  mental and emotional, 14
    anger, 45
    constant wariness, 49
    counseling for, 50
    crying, 45
    on families and friends of victims, 45–46, 48
    grief, 47
    lifelong terror, 43–44
    moral injury, 50
    numbness, 45
  physical, 49, 51
    rehabilitation, 43, 46
    research needed, 50
El Salvador, 11
entertainment venues, mass shootings at, 26, 27–28, 58
Everytown for Gun Safety, 55

Fabio, Anthony, 16
Falkowski, Melissa, 45
family members
  domestic violence, 7, 23–25, **24**
  effects on, of victims, 44, 45–46, 47–48
FBI, background checks by, 13, 17, 54
Feinstein, Dianne, 62–63
Finland, 27
Finner, Troy, 19
Firearms Act (1995, Canada), 14
First Baptist Church (Sutherland Springs, Texas), 17
Florida, 55
France, 27
Franklin, Richard, 60–61
Frazier, Erica, 4
French, David, 11
fully automatic weapons, 60

Galea, Sandro, 14
gang violence, homicides related to, 19–20
gender
  deaths from interpersonal conflicts and, 22–23, 25
  gun suicide and, 35–36
  gun violence and, 36
Germany, 8, 27
Giffords Law Center to Prevent Gun Violence, 59
Global Terrorism Database (University of Maryland), 27
Graduate Institute of International and Development Studies (Geneva, Switzerland), 9

Greensboro, North Carolina, 5
Greer, Kimberly, 46–48
Greer, Ricky, 47
Greer, Ryann, 46
Gresham, Oregon, 4
Gross, Dan, 31

handguns
   age for purchase of, 12, 55
   background checks and, 54
   damage inflicted and caliber of, 62
   storage of, 56–57, 58–59
Harvard T.H. Chan School of Public Health, 30–31
Harvard University, 10
Hawaii, 55, 63
Hempstead, Katherine, 31
high-capacity magazines, 63
high-tech sensor locks, 59–60
Hispanics, 20, 37
Holtzman, Allen, 37
Hooks, Pamela Crumpton, 5
hospitalizations, 14
Houston, Texas, 19
Hunt, Amber, 51

Idaho, 35
illegal guns, most begin with legal ownership, 16
Illinois, 55
India, 8
injuries, 14
   Las Vegas Route 91 Harvest music festival (2017), 27, 58
   May 18–19, 2018, 4–5
   Orlando, Florida Pulse nightclub (2016), 28
   rape, 42–44
   robbery, 48–49
Institute for Health Metrics and Evaluation (University of Washington), 8
interpersonal conflicts
   domestic violence, 7, 23–25, **24**
   between family members, 23
   gender and, 22–23, 25

JAMA Network Open, 62
James, Alexa, 50
James, Thea, 14

Johnson, Susan, 48
Johnson, Trae, 22
Jones, Benedict, 51
Journal of the American Medical Association (*JAMA*), 8, 52, 58

Kelley, Devin P., 17
Knopov, Anita, 29

Lane, Joel, 23–25
Lane, Michelle, 23–25
Lankford, Adam, 25–26
Las Vegas, Nevada, 27, 58
Latino Americans, 20, 37
Lexington, Kentucky, 23
Liggins, Jordan "BayBay," 47
Long, Ian David, 26
long guns, age for purchase of, 12
Lott, John R., Jr., 26–27
Louis Armstrong New Orleans International Airport, 41

Mack, De'Lindsey Dwayne, 19
Marjory Stoneman Douglas High School (Parkland, Florida), 28, **28**, 45
Marrero, Louisiana, 4
Maryland
   assault weapons bans, 63
   background checks, 54
Massachusetts
   assault weapons bans, 63
   safety devices on and storage of guns in, 57, 58–59
mass shootings
   during church services, 17
   definition of, 25
   at entertainment venues, 26, 27–28, 58
   as percent of gun homicides, 29
   percent of world, in US, 25–27
   at schools, 4, **28**, 28–29, 45, 53
mental health, 12, 14
Mokdad, Ali, 8
Montana, 35
Moody, Wintez Ta'Vorius, 22
moral injury, 50
Mumbai, India, 26

Naib, Cayman, 30
Naib, Farid, 30

National Firearms Agreement (1996, Australia), 60–61
National Instant Criminal Background Check System (NICS), 13, 17, 54
National Institutes of Health (NIH), 53
National Rifle Association (NRA), contributions to political campaigns by, 18
Native Americans, firearm suicide rate, 38
NBC News, 10
New Jersey, assault weapons bans, 63
New Orleans, Louisiana, 41
Newtown, Connecticut, 28, 53
New York, 57, 63
non-Hispanic whites, 20, 37, 38–39
Norway, 27

Obama, Barrack, 20, 53, **54**
O.F. Mossberg & Sons, 59, 60
Orfanos, Marc, 26
Orfanos, Telemachus "Tel," 26
Orlando, Florida, 28
ownership of guns
    in Canada, 13–14
    legal restrictions on
        age and, 12, 55
        overview, 12
        by people with dementia, 37
        US politics and, 16–18
    most illegal guns begin as legal, 16
    percent of US households, 35
    roots of culture of, 11–12
    suicide and, 33–35
    truthfulness of surveys about, 10–11

Pacific Islanders, firearm suicide rate, 38
Pagourtzis, Dimitrios, 4
Pahn, Molly, 29
Parkland, Florida, 28, **28,** 45
Pennsylvania, background checks, 54
Pew Research Center, 11, 15
Philippines, 27
physicians, role of, in reducing access to guns, 39
Pike, Christopher, 4
Pittman, Billy, 42–43, 44
protection, as reason for owning gun, 11

Protection of Lawful Commerce in Arms Act (2005), 56–57
public health policy, effect of statistics on, 41
Public Safety and Recreational Firearms Use Protection Act (1994), 61–62
Pulse nightclub (Orlando, Florida), 28

race
    homicide rates, 20–21
    suicide rates and, 37–39
    See also African Americans
Ramirez, Brenda, 44–46
Ramirez, Emely, 44–46
Reagan, Ronald, 62
Reese, Carol, 50
religion and suicides, 11
research, 50, 52–53
Rothman, Emily F., 35
Route 91 Harvest music festival (Las Vegas, Nevada), 27, 58
Russia, 27

safety courses, 14, **15**
safety measures
    age restrictions, 12, 55–56
    assault weapons ban, 60–63
    background checks, 13, 17, 53–55
    criminal history, 12
    high-capacity magazine ban, 63
    high-tech sensor locks, 59–60
    mental health issues, 12
    reducing firepower of handguns, 62
    research and, 52–53
    trigger locks/guards, 30, 56–59, **57**
sale of guns
    availability, **10**
    background checks and, 13, 17, 53–55
    Dallas Gun Show, **13**
    restrictions on, 12, 55–56
Sandy Hook Elementary School (Newtown, Connecticut), 28, 53
Santa Fe High School (Texas), 4, 28
Sauk City, Wisconsin, 4
Schmidt-Orfanos, Susan, 26
schools, mass shootings at, 4, **28,** 28–29, 45, 53
semiautomatic weapons, 60–63, **61**

sensor locks, 59–60
Shine, Jeffrey, 48–49
Siegel, Michael, 29, 35
Small Arms Survey, 9
state laws
   assault weapons bans, 63
   background checks, 54–55
   minimum age for purchase of guns, 12, 55
   See also specific states
statistics and public health policy, 41
Stolbach, Brad, 46
Studdert, David, 7, 41
suicides
   age and, 39–40, 56
   availability of guns and, 33–35
   bullying and, 33
   decision to commit, 30, 40, 56
   failed attempts, 32
   gender and, 35–36
   high-tech sensor locks and, 59
   increase in, 31
   number of guns and, 9
   as percent of gun deaths, 6
   as preventable, 31–32
   race and, 37–39
   reducing firearm, 39
   religion and, 11
   as second-leading nondisease cause of death, 31
   successful, after failed attempts, 30–31
   by teens, 59
   trigger locks and safe storage and, 56
Sutherland Springs, Texas, 17
Switzerland, 10

Tabak, Lawrence, 53
Thousand Oaks, California, 26
trigger locks/guards, 30, 56–59, **57**
Trump, Donald, 53
Tulsa, Oklahoma, 4–5
2017, 5

United Kingdom, 8, 27
United States
   changing culture in, 39
   number of guns in, 9
   number of guns stolen annually in, 10
   percent of households in, with guns, 10–11
   percent of world mass shootings in, 25–27
   protests against gun violence in, **47**
   rate of gun deaths per 100,000 people, 8
   See also Congress
University of Colorado–Denver, 34
University of Maryland, 27
University of Pittsburgh, 16, 60
University of Washington, 8, 36
University of Washington–Seattle, 56
US Department of Defense, 17
US Government Accountability Office, 56

Vela, Brandy, 33
Vela, Jacqueline, 33
Vela, Raul, 33
Venezuela, 11
Violent Crime Control and Law Enforcement Act (1994), 18
Virginia Polytechnic Institute and State University (Blacksburg, Virginia), 28–29

Wall Street Journal (newspaper), 10
Washington Post (newspaper), 27
Webster, Daniel W.
   on reducing firearm suicides, 39
   on relationship between number of guns and gun deaths and suicides, 9
   on risk associated with guns in house, 36
   on suicide as preventable, 31–32
Wintemute, Garen, 40
Wisconsin, 20, 21
workplace violence, deaths from, 7
Wyoming, 17–18, 35

Zogby Analytics, 11

PICTURE CREDITS

Cover: Sascha Burkard/Shutterstock.com

6: Maury Aaseng
10: WKanadapon/Shutterstock.com
13: Tian Dan Xinhua News Agency/Newscom
15: Robert Przybysz/Shutterstock.com
21: galubovystock/Shutterstock.com
24: lolfilolo/DepositPhotos
28: Janos Rautonen/Shutterstock.com
32: Antonio Guillem/Shutterstock.com
34: DmitriMaruta/iStockphoto.com
38: Rob Hainer/Shutterstock.com
42: Peerayut Chan/Shutterstock.com
47: Nicole S Glass/Shutterstock.com
48: Monkey Business Images/Shutterstock.com
54: Joseph Sohm/Shutterstock.com
57: iStockphoto.com
61: artas/iStockphoto.com